Tell Me Everything

Tell

Me

Everything

CAROLYN COMAN

Farrar, Straus & Giroux

New York

For my mother and father
Nathalie and Edward Coman

Tell Me Everything

One

Roz imagined herself a statue—pure, white stone. At the back of the classroom, Mrs. Grafton aimed the video camera. In five separate rows of four, her classmates sat waiting for Roz to begin. She held perfectly still.

"Remember," Mrs. Grafton called out, "nice and loud so we can all hear."

Roz looked down at the index cards she held in her hand. Remember, she told herself. Remember what? She willed her mouth to open and begin her first oral report since entering sixth grade at the Middle School in Newburyport.

"Ellie Jacoby went up in a burst of flames," she started. Her throat was dry as crumpled paper.

"Louder, please," Mrs. Grafton urged.

"A burst of flames," Roz said again, at double the volume. Saying it so much louder made it sound terribly true. "She died on board the *Challenger* with the whole world watching. It was on the TV news, the rocket exploding. It looked like fireworks, all the fragments in the sky."

Roz paused and went to her next index card, studied it for a moment, and said, "The people on the ground who were watching got sore necks from tilting their heads back for so long, but they couldn't stop looking. Even after it got dark, they kept staring into the sky. They wanted to put the pieces back together, like they tried to do with Humpty Dumpty. But Ellie Jacoby was gone. She was a heroine. The President said so."

Her mouth shut tight, and without lifting her head, Roz raised her eyes to see Mrs. Grafton. The room was completely quiet.

"Roz?" Mrs. Grafton asked. "Is that all?" She spoke very softly.

Roz nodded. Mrs. Grafton clicked off the camera, set it down, and began walking toward the front of the room. Roz's classmates twisted in their seats, watching to see what Mrs. Grafton would do. Scott Ventrow called out, "*Who* got blasted?"

"Scott." Mrs. Grafton practically spat his name, and he slumped down in his desk and kicked the seat in front of him.

Mrs. Grafton walked up beside Roz and placed a hand on her back. She looked down at the note cards Roz held, the one on top completely filled with an explosion of bright colored lines. Mrs. Grafton reached down and gently took them from Roz, lifting the top card to see the ones beneath it. The first showed cartoon faces in profile, all of the heads tilted back, their elongated noses pointing up to the sky. The next one showed Humpty Dumpty off his wall and hitting the ground, zigzag cracks all through him. Mrs. Grafton handed the cards back and said, "We'll talk after class, Roz. You can sit down now."

Scott tried again. "What about questions?" he called out. "Who'd she say died?" Mrs. Grafton ignored him and called on Jessica Winowski to report next.

Roz willed life into her stone-statue legs and walked back to her seat. Her classmates tittered like birds around her, and Roz remembered how the birds sounded—how much noise they made when they started waking up—when she was little and slept out with her mother in a tent.

She poured herself into the memory and rode it like a wave, away from the tinny, empty feeling school gave her—the way a locker door sounded when it slammed. As if the door were slamming on her, and she were left, stuffed into that thin dark locker, let out only at someone else's whim. As if there might not be quite enough air to breathe, and no real way to turn around or move her body.

While Jessica Winowski began her report on Mother Teresa, Roz went back to the North Country—her first home—and climbed inside the tent, beside her mother. There was a particular filtered light that came through the orange nylon at dawn. Cocooned in her sleeping bag, Roz let the light permeate the tent before she rose up on her elbow to see whether her mother was there or not.

The bell clamored the end of class—time to shift to another classroom, another teacher—and Roz's heart raced. Jessica wasn't standing at the front of the room anymore. It was Dennis Landry, rushing through to the ·end of his report on Martin Luther King, Jr. The bell always came as a surprise to Roz, out of nowhere and loud and sudden, as if something were wrong, as if there were some emergency.

Mrs. Grafton motioned to her to stay put. The others filed past into the hallway.

"Was your report about your mother, Roz?" Mrs. Grafton asked, once the room had emptied.

"Yes," she said.

Mrs. Grafton folded her hands together and Roz watched her painted nails settle over her knuckles. She did not speak for a minute. "And you said that she died on *Challenger*? The space shuttle?" Their class had watched the whole story—the lift-off, the explosion, the memorial service—on television the month before.

Roz did not answer. She appreciated the ring of oval jewels Mrs. Grafton's nails made around her hands.

"Did you understand the assignment, Roz? An oral report on a hero or heroine?"

Mrs. Grafton sounded, to Roz, like she wasn't really sure of what she was saying. Roz's heart went out to her.

"Roz?" Mrs. Grafton said again.

"Yes?"

"Are you listening to me?"

"Yes," Roz told her, because she was. Just then she was listening very hard.

"This was supposed to be a non-fiction report," Mrs. Grafton continued, looking at Roz as if she were a little scared. Roz watched her closely. "Non-fiction means something that actually happened, a real event involving real people. Remember how we talked about the main characteristics of expository writing and speaking? Remember FIRE?"

Roz nodded. She remembered fire.

"And do you remember what FIRE stands for?" Roz could feel Mrs. Grafton wanting to pull something out of her, but she didn't have it in her to give.

"Remember?" she asked again. "Facts. Incidents. Reasons." She stopped there, as though she might have cranked up Roz's memory by giving her the first three answers. But Roz stood silent in front of her and finally Mrs. Grafton finished, saying, "Examples."

They faced each other, and then Mrs. Grafton repeated the words, fast this time. "Facts, Incidents, Reasons, Examples. FIRE. We went over those, Roz, remember?"

Roz remembered the stories her mother read to her, and talked about: Mary and Martha, Abraham and Isaac, doubting Thomas, the miracle of the loaves and fishes. Did those stories have fire? "I don't know," she finally said, and when Mrs. Grafton did not say anything else, Roz asked her, "Should I go to social studies now?"

Mrs. Grafton took a small step back from Roz and breathed out. "Yes," she said, "yes, I'll write you a pass."

Mrs. McCaffey had already begun by the time Roz got to her classroom. Roz stood outside the door and listened in. "You cannot imagine," Mrs. McCaffey instructed the class—as if it were an order—"the importance of natural resources." Roz entered the classroom. She placed the pass on Mrs. McCaffey's desk and then made her way to the back row, where she always sat. When she walked by Scott Ventrow, he made a funny sound, maybe just clearing his throat, but not really—more like a little explosion going off. It reverberated inside Roz's head, even as she sat down and pulled out her social studies book and turned to the right page. The noise kept playing in her head, until finally she shot him a look—one that, in total silence, would make him stop. Scott was not looking her way, though. He was leaning forward, dragging his eraser across his desk top, drawing in faint pink lines, and his mouth was closed. Roz dropped her head, setting off still another explosion. She was afraid. She held perfectly still and tried to empty every sound in the world out of her, so that the noise would stop. Sometime during class, it did.

At two twenty-five, after the final bell, Roz stood by her locker, sardined among everyone else getting ready to leave, choosing the books she needed for homework. A low, guttural chant finally pushed its way into her hearing: "Ja-co-by, Ja-co-by." She looked down the hall until she found Scott drum-beating out her name. The instant her eyes met his, he held up his inflated paper bag from lunch, choking it at the neck with one hand. In a split second he had smacked it flat, exploded it. He laughed and turned away.

She placed all her books back in her locker and then closed the door, lifting up the latch so it wouldn't make a noise. Roz was a big girl, and older than most of her classmates, since she'd been held back a year when she'd arrived in Newburyport the previous October. She had a certain grace, though—a bearing—that up to that moment had kept the other kids from both mocking and approaching her. She walked down to Scott, whose back was to her, and stood behind him, still as a deer. When he turned around, she swung and hit him full in the face.

Her fist connected with his left cheek and then up across the bridge of his nose. The shock of being hit, even more than the force of her blow, knocked him off his balance and back against his locker. His mouth fell open in disbelief. Roz watched it drop open, and it seemed that punching him had made him younger—knocked some years off him, somehow—because what she was seeing was a scared little boy, falling backward away from her. Then all she wanted to do was reach out and save him, but it was too late.

She felt the impact of the hit all through her. She shook her hand, but could not shake off the feeling of her fist against his face, the skin and bones of it, the clank of her knuckles against him, the giving way. It was as if her hand had already memorized the feeling forever.

There were kids all around them, and, after just a second of dead silence, a burst of excited noise engulfed her. Scott was standing, his face scrunched up, mad, trying not to cry. He made no move to hit her back. Suddenly Mr. Renard, the vice-principal, landed among them, as if he'd been hurtled from the other end of the hallway.

He was in a hurry to do something, Roz could tell. There was nothing for him to do, though. Everything was over. He scanned the faces shouting out to him, but Scott, with his messed hair and pounding red blotch on the left side of his face, was the only obvious culprit. Mr. Renard raised his hand to silence the noise—"Spare me," he said—and then dropped it heavily on Scott's shoulder.

"I hit him," Roz said. She did not speak loudly, but her voice was clear and rang out. She remembered: nice and loud so we can all hear.

Everyone turned to look at her—just as they had in class, waiting for her to begin her report—and she again willed herself to hold still and look at Mr. Renard. Mr. Renard returned her stare, mute for just a moment, as if he had not heard her correctly. Roz held his eyes, though, and he finally said to both Scott and her, "Come with me." They followed him down the hall, away from the others who called out after them, "He didn't do anything." "She started it." "Jacoby ambushed him."

Roz stretched out the fingers of her hand as she walked just a little behind and to the right of Mr. Renard. Scott walked on Mr. Renard's left, and Roz could see that the years she'd knocked off him were coming back. He didn't look like a little boy anymore. He wasn't about to cry, and he walked as though he'd been the one who'd thrown the punch. She opened her palm flat and tried to make the feeling, the memory of the hit, slide off its smooth surface. They entered Mr. Renard's office and he closed the door behind them. She willed the memory to exit out her stretched fingers, but nothing budged.

Her mother's hands, kneading dough, were long and thin and strong. They could hold, and mold, almost anything. From the time she was little, Roz had made bread with her mother, rolling the dough in a dusting of flour on the thick, slightly sagging wooden table in their kitchen. After it had risen for the first time, her mother would stand up on her tiptoes and lean her whole body weight into the ball of dough, punching out the air with both fists so that it exhaled a little gasp, and then settle into the rhythmic pressing and folding, first pushing the dough away from her, and then drawing it back toward her.

She taught Roz just how to do it. She stood behind her daughter and placed her long hands over Roz's short, plump little-girl hands, guiding her until their rhythm and motion were one. In just remembering, Roz could feel the dough, its lump as she dragged it across the film of flour her mother sprinkled on the tabletop, its smooth face—"like a baby's bottom," her mother said—how it totally gave way when she punched her fist into its freshly risen surface. Mr. Renard talked away.

"In-house suspension," he finished. "This behavior cannot and will not be tolerated." She watched his mouth work as he spoke—he had a funny way of pinching his lips together, as if everything he said was escaping from him—but all she heard was that one word: *suspension*. She liked the sound of it. Suspended was how she often felt, though she hadn't, until then, had a name for it.

She remembered the suspension bridge that she and her mother crossed to reach one of their favorite, most secret places to camp. It was a swinging, wooden-planked bridge, over a rock-lined stream, connecting two strips of land overgrown with lush summer green. Crossing it had both frightened and thrilled her. It was such a midair feeling: to walk on something so free that it moved with the weather and her own movements. She watched each wooden plank intensely as she stepped on it, and had no sense at all of moving forward until she was actually setting foot on solid ground again.

She pictured herself suspended at school. She saw herself floating vertically down the hallways, hovering just slightly above the buffed linoleum floors. That was punishment? Mr. Renard asked her if she had anything to say for herself, but she couldn't imagine what it might be.

"Then have I made myself perfectly clear?" Mr. Renard wanted to know next. He had bent down so that he was eye to eye with Roz. She *hoped* that he had, with all the talking he'd done. It seemed clear to her that she was the wrong person to ask, since she hadn't been listening, but she gave him the benefit of the doubt and told him, "Yes."

He seemed relieved to hear it—he dropped his shoul-

ders a few inches, and lowered his voice—and then told
her to wait on the bench outside the administrative offices
while he tried, once again, to reach her uncle by phone.
She sat in the empty hallway, hooking her fingers around
the rim of the seat and resting the tops of her sneakers
on the bar that ran below it, so that her body leaned
forward, out into the slightly darkened hall. She closed
her eyes. No prayer filled her—none had for months,
not since she'd come to Newburyport—but for just a
moment she had the faraway feeling her mother always
told her came from resting in the hand of God. She tried
to hold on to it, but it washed over her and then away.

She sat in the hallway a long time, and nothing happened and no one came. She wondered about Scott. It
occurred to her, for just a second, that perhaps he had
vanished. She knew better—or at least different; she
knew that he hadn't vanished, and that she would face
him in school again and again. It didn't matter, though,
whether he was there or not, because her hand remembered everything.

Mr. Renard finally appeared. He motioned to her as
if he were directing traffic, and she rose and stepped inside
his office. Scott sat in a cafeteria chair against the wall.
She wondered if he had been there the whole time. She
only remembered seeing him walking down the hall as
though he had thrown the first punch, any punch. He
did not look at her, just smacked the heel of his sneaker
against the chrome leg of the chair. One dark lock of
black hair fell across his forehead.

"Roz," Mr. Renard said, "I have not been able to reach
your uncle. The front office does not have a completed
form from you, on whom to call in case of emergency."

Emergency.

He handed her a pink rectangle of heavy paper. "Please have your uncle fill this out tonight, and return it to me personally tomorrow morning, before you report for in-house suspension." Roz held the paper in her hand and did not say a word. "Before I release you, then, there's just one other matter to take care of."

Care. Matter. Release.

He looked toward Scott. "You owe Scott an apology, Rosalind," he said. "Wouldn't you agree?" He stepped next to Scott and, by placing his hand on the boy's back, encouraged him to stand up and step toward Roz.

"Rosalind?" Mr. Renard said. "We're waiting."

No one called her Rosalind. "What are we waiting for?" she finally asked.

Mr. Renard pulled back from her just slightly, the way Mrs. Grafton had. His face went blank for a second and then his eyebrows pulled toward each other and he tilted his head as he studied her. "We're waiting for your apology to Scott," he said, flat, no-nonsense.

"Oh!" Roz said. "Oh." She turned to face Scott, extended her hand, the one that had hit him, the one that remembered, and said, "I'm sorry, Scott. From the bottom of my heart."

They just popped out—the words her mother spoke every night. "I love you, darling. From the bottom of my heart." Roz loved those words, and it felt so good to hear them again, even if she was the one saying them.

Scott gave her a confused, embarrassed look and briefly grazed his hand against hers before turning away. "Can I *go* now?" he said.

"Yes," Mr. Renard said. He was watching Roz. "Yes, you can both go now."

She went back to her locker and retrieved the books

she had so carefully set down before she slugged Scott. She packed the pile into her knapsack and held it against her chest, and then closed the door quietly again. She heard a slam all the same. A slam and then an explosion.

So slugging Scott Ventrow had done nothing, she realized—no good at all, because the exploding sound had gone inside her, and now it erupted in a corridor empty as a bubble.

She left school and headed straight for the pay phone near the intersection of High and State. She did not think about where she was going, or what she was going to do when she got there. She just went, a dog on scent, following a track that led only one place. As soon as the phone booth came into her line of vision, she shoved her hand deep into her pocket and wrapped her fingers around the handful of quarters and dimes she always carried with her.

Roz started feeding change into the black box almost before she stopped walking. She pushed the last nickel into the slot and waited for the phone to digest it. She listened to all the clicks and then the quiet. An operator thanked her for using AT&T, and Roz said, "You're welcome." A few seconds later the phone in New Jersey began to ring. Her hands got sweaty, like always. Four rings. Five. At least if no one answered she'd get her money back, all those quarters and dimes and nickels pouring back into the silver cup marked RETURN. Six rings. Seven.

"Hullo?"

It was him, she knew—Nate, the boy her mother had died for. She knew that quick, dumb-sounding way he had of saying hello. As if he'd just run in from somewhere and tripped over his own clumsy feet getting to the phone. Roz wasn't breathing.

"Hullo?" he said, louder, and then nothing at all: they just listened to each other listening. He must know, Roz thought. She was sure she could feel him get a little afraid.

She heard him *hmmph*, pushing a breath out his nose, like he wasn't a bit scared, just bothered, and then he hung up, and then Roz did, and the phone swallowed all her change for the final time, as if the meal was over. Her heart was pumping; it always did after she called Nate, but she knew no one could see that. She knew she looked just like any other twelve-year-old girl, a girl large for her age, with straight blond hair and broad shoulders, a girl in jeans and a blue sweater and sneakers, stepping away from the pay phone near the intersection of High and State, on her way home from the Middle School.

She swung her backpack over her shoulder and started walking, on another track that only led home. As she approached Greenleaf Street, she got the same relieved feeling she always did after making one of her "scary phone calls"—that was how she described them to herself, though she wasn't exactly sure who they scared besides her—she got the feeling that it would hold her for a while.

No sign marked Roz's street—Greenleaf. The road just curved off State Street, on its way up to the big graveyard, Oak Hill. Mike's house, the smaller of the only two homes on the left, was set farther back, partially hidden by a tangle of overgrown forsythia bushes and shade trees.

She cut across the brown grass of their never-mowed lawn, hopped onto the granite slab step, and pushed open the front door. Joan, Roz's dog, had her strong, bony head against Roz's thigh the instant she stepped inside, into the dark, rich oil and gas smells that permeated Mike's entire downstairs. Mike fixed things, in the living room that over the past few years had turned into his shop. She bent over, nuzzling. "Joan, good Joan."

She loved how Mike's house smelled, different as it was from Jefferson, where it was the wood stove and her mother's baking that scented everything. Roz felt guilty at how easily she had switched over to Mike's house, to his smells, after only five months. As if she hadn't loved her mother's house, or hadn't loved it enough.

She sidestepped an outboard motor stored in the hallway and walked into the shop. Mike had a squat, white appliance up on his workbench, the Little Baker.

"*That* makes bread?" she asked, plopping down onto the couch. Clotted stuffing poked out from the cushions. It was hard for her to believe about the white metal thing, so unlike hands.

"When it works," he said. "How was school?"

He asked every day, even though Roz knew he didn't want to hear any more than she wanted to tell.

"Where were you before?" she said.

He looked at her. "Out on a pickup," he said. Mike loved making pickups and deliveries, didn't even charge for them. "Why?"

Roz didn't answer for a second, then said, "Mr. Renard tried to call you. He called me Rosalind." She rested her chin on the tops of her knees. "Doesn't that sound queer—Rosalind?"

"Who's Mr. Renard?" Mike said.

"Vice-principal." She'd started picking at the cracking rubber of her sneaker toe. "He pinches his words."

Mike turned from the workbench to look at Roz.

She pursed her lips and said very distinctly, one word at a time, "We're. Waiting. Rosalind."

Mike laughed, waited.

"You know how you can feel the eye socket and the cheek and everything?" she said.

Mike leaned against his bench. "When?"

"When you punch someone in the face," she said.

He sighed, ran his hand over his thinly covered scalp. Roz assumed Mike knew about fighting. He was a man. He'd been in Vietnam. "Isn't it disgusting?" she said. Her hand was remembering.

Mike nodded without speaking. All he finally said was "Anyone get hurt?"

Roz placed her hand flat on the couch and looked down at it. "Yes," she said, feeling, all of a sudden, how much it *had* hurt—how *hurt* was exactly the word for it, all of it—before and during, and after, too, when she could not forget it.

It occurred to Roz then that Mike might have meant, *Did it hurt Scott?*

"Oh, it must have," she said. "It had to." She remembered the way not crying had twisted his face. "I mean, I'm sure it hurt him, too."

Mike went back to the appliance. "Are we talking trouble here?" he said.

"Suspension," Roz said, holding on to the end of the word as if it had a tail.

"Aw, Roz," Mike said, disappointed. "Goddammit."

Roz loved the way Mike swore. He was the first person she knew who blasphemed, who took words she knew so well and used them so differently, and he had a gentle, almost appreciative way of doing it.

He started zapping the TV in the corner of the room with the remote control. She knew he dreaded dealing with the school, with what he called the authorities. Mike hated official business. When he'd registered Roz at the Middle School in October—the first school outside her mother's house that she'd ever been to—she'd watched deep stains soak the sides of his shirt.

"Oh, well," he said, after a minute, "it'll blow over" —his version of what her mother often said: "This, too, shall pass."

"I guess," Roz said. She didn't tell him that every time he said it, she pictured a funnel of twirling wind, blowing like mad, coming straight at them.

"Who hit who?" Mike said.

"I hit him, I hit Scott," she remembered. "He didn't believe my report on Mom."

"You gave a report on Ellie? What'd you say?"

"I said she blew up on board the *Challenger*, blew to smithereens with the whole world watching."

"You did?"

"Now they're scared of me." She saw Scott's face, against the locker, trying not to cry, and Mrs. Grafton pulling back from her, just a breath. "They think I don't know what happened."

"Well," Mike said, reaching around and pressing his wide palm against the back of his neck, rubbing it hard, "it's not exactly what'd I'd call the hard-boiled truth." He gave Roz a slightly apologetic shrug, as if he was sorry he had to say so.

Roz liked what he'd said, though: "hard-boiled truth"—she said it inside her head, to print it there. She pictured a hard-boiled egg, just peeled, so shiny it looked wet, and she thought about the funny way it felt—not hard at all. She saw Humpty Dumpty, falling. "Who cares if she wasn't the exact person who blew up on the spaceship?" she asked Mike. It all felt the same to Roz. Her mother always told her, when she read to her from the Bible, "It's the heart of the story that matters." At least with the *Challenger*, Roz could watch what happened; she could watch it over and over, on instant replay, if she needed to. For a second she felt out of the shop, away from Mike, and back in school, with hardly enough air to breathe.

Mike sighed. "But teachers are bound to get nervous if you go making claims you can't sub-stan-ti-ate." Whenever he used a word that he knew was particularly correct, he sounded it out that way to her, syllable by syllable.

Roz sighed, sorry for the whole business.

"It'll blow over," Mike told her again. "You want something to eat?"

"No," Roz said. "I'm gonna walk Joan." Joan sprang up from Roz's feet at the word *walk* and trotted to the door. Joan had been her mother's dog (Ellie Jacoby had answered an ad in the local paper that said "Want a Big Dog?") and Roz had inherited her. She looked to be part greyhound, part Irish wolfhound, short-haired, honey-colored, tall and lean. In Jefferson, Roz had seen Joan run so fast that she disappeared into a blur, a streaking missile that Roz's eyes couldn't track. Ellie had called her the dog of her dreams.

"We'll be back," Roz told Mike, and she and Joan walked out to the road that led up to the graveyard— Roz's favorite place to go. She walked there at least once a day, sometimes more, and the place, even though it was a cemetery, never spooked her.

There were always plenty of sticks to throw for Joan in

among the gravestones. Roz had a good arm. She pitched a branch for Joan to chase, and followed up behind her, reading the tombstones as she walked by them. One of her favorites was a tall stone marker for someone named Daniel Hamilton, with a sculpted hand on it, set back just a few yards from the main path. All the fingers were closed into a fist, except for the pointer finger, which shot straight up toward the sky. Underneath the hand it said: GONE TO HEAVEN. Roz loved how clear it all was, chiseled into the stone, pointing the way, sure of itself.

Some of the inscriptions were hard to make out, worn down by time and weather, or covered by yellow or green fungus. It mattered to Roz, though, what they said, and she spent time making out the letters and dates. Sometimes she even bent down and traced the inscriptions with her finger, to help her feel what they had to say, almost as if she were blind.

Roz liked the inscriptions that told her something about the person—more than the words about God and his love that most people had chiseled below their names and dates. She felt bad about her preference, because she was pretty sure that her mother would want some God words on her marker.

After Roz's mom died, she'd been cremated, and there had been talk of scattering her ashes on the mountain where she'd died. The community wanted to honor what they saw as Ellie's act of heroism—the same community that had called her crazy when she was alive. It was the one time during the week of gatherings and services that Roz had spoken up about what she wanted, and it had surprised everybody when she said what was on her mind. After the accident, she was silent, and different people were sent to try and coax a word out of her—a minister with puffy white hands from one of the churches in Lancaster; and Mrs. Brummel, their closest neighbor, though they rarely saw her; even a child, a delicate girl Roz's own age named Kate, whom Roz would have known had she attended the public school, who in a different world could have been Roz's best friend. With each of them, the more Roz was quiet, the more they talked. So it came out of the blue when, after Mike arrived and they were discussing what to do with the ashes, Roz said, "Give them to me. I want them." It had even surprised Roz. She hadn't known she wanted the ashes, or what in the world she might do with them. But it was the one and only thing she had asked for, and she'd been given them, and brought them back down to Newburyport with her, and put them in her closet, where they now were. Sometimes, when she walked Joan in the graveyard, she studied the tombstones all around her to see what other people had done with their leftovers. Her very favorite stone was the one for Sara Worthington Curtis, whose inscription read: A TRUE WOMAN.

Roz followed Joan into a protected spot—a cradle of land, almost—and then squatted down and dropped onto her back on the grass. She stretched her hands out beneath her head and crossed her ankles. Joan took it as a signal to race off, up the hill and out of sight, but Roz knew she'd be back.

Roz didn't go to the graveyard to walk so much as she went to watch and listen. She went always to the same spot, where the branches of two big trees stretched out and marked off a chunk of the sky. Their limbs made it into a screen, or a rink, or a playing field, where she could inspect whatever came sailing through. There was nothing dreamy about it for Roz. She watched intently

—ready, even, for a heron to swoop out of nowhere, blocking out the sky with its wide-stretched wings. That had happened one time, in Jefferson, with her mother: a blue heron came flying low across the road, out of nowhere, out of the past, and her mother had told Roz it was a sure sign.

Ever since she'd come to Newburyport, Roz had been waiting and hoping for a sure sign. As sure as the heron, or thunder in the middle of a snowstorm—she'd had that too, with her mother, during a March blizzard, in the field behind their house—or a fox. Her mother spotted foxes all the time in the North Country, but Roz never looked up in time, or followed her mother's pointing finger fast enough. She worried about the number of signs she might already have missed. And she wondered, when you finally do get one, is it crystal clear what you're supposed to do? These were questions that hadn't come up when Ellie was alive. Roz had never needed to ask because Ellie always knew. On her own, Roz could not be sure about what the signs were and how, exactly, they worked—only that they mattered.

She hoped, deep down, for something from above, and that was why she watched the sky. Even after the cold crept into her back, like the memory of winter pushing up from the ground, she still did not move. She was waiting for a sign from God, or from her mother, who was with God.

After a while, Joan came back and licked her face. Roz hoped that she had waited long enough, that a sign would not appear behind her back as soon as she stood and turned away, and she pulled herself up and they went home.

Mike was working on veal parmigiana for dinner. "Be

ready in about half an hour," he told her. He dropped a cutlet onto a plate of flour, and the littlest poof of white rose up. "Why not take a stab at your homework?" Usually he didn't mention it one way or the other.

After dinner, they went into the shop and turned on the TV. Roz was still getting used to TV in her life— she and Ellie hadn't had one up in Jefferson. Now, every night, she and Mike cruised the tube. Left to herself, Roz would have settled into just one of the stories they zipped by. It was hard on her to be given only a snatch of dialogue, a look, someone tumbling off a window ledge. She felt obliged to imagine what had started it, who was losing what, the love that was there, to get to some sort of ending. But Mike kept up a pretty regular beat with punching the channels.

He flipped to 54 and held still longer than usual. Roz couldn't even tell what the story was at first, just all these rubber-gloved hands. Finally the commentator's English voice told them that it was open-heart surgery. Even knowing, Roz recognized nothing, no heart she'd ever seen.

Mike kind of snorted when the voice started listing the massive expenses involved in operations "of this nature." Mike had been a medic in Vietnam. "You can stop the bleeding for a lot less than that," he told the TV.

"You *did* that?" Roz said.

"I did open-chest work," he said. "But not like that. I used stuff like cellophane off a pack of cigarettes to stop the bleeding." After another minute, he switched over to MTV.

Roz couldn't get the picture out of her head, though: Mike sticking his hands inside someone's chest, reaching right inside a wound, laying his hands on whatever he was supposed to connect or cut out. She kept hoping he would click back to the operation, so she could see the whole man—or maybe it was a woman—and hear from the doctor about how it felt to do that.

"Was it like Thomas?" she finally just asked Mike, after he didn't go back.

"Thomas?"

"In the Bible," she said. "You know—Jesus' friend, who couldn't believe Jesus rose from the dead until he touched the places where Jesus had been nailed to the cross. Then he finally believed."

Mike scratched the back of his head. "It was my job, Roz," he said. "I can't say that it helped me believe."

She wasn't listening, though. She was picturing Thomas, who looked just like Mike. And she could see how reaching out like that—actually touching the wound—could help someone believe.

Two

Roz got her nightmare later than usual that
night. Light was already breaking through when Mike
shook her awake and told her she'd had another bad
dream, to come on down to the kitchen and he'd make
her some hot cocoa. He yanked her out of sleep once or
twice a week, away from some dream that he said made
her holler. All Roz ever remembered was Mike's voice
rousing her, telling her it was okay, everything was okay.

She pulled herself out of bed as if she were hauling
her body up from another world. It was so hard coming
back from sleep, even to be saved, even for something
that she wanted—the way she felt when Ellie shook her
awake to see the northern lights. Ellie woke Roz on the
nights they camped out in the field behind their house,
whenever the northern lights put on a show. But more
than the lights themselves, Roz remembered the tug to
pull herself away from sleep and dreams. The next morning, she was never sure if she had seen the streaks of

white across the sky, or simply dreamed them. Ellie told Roz that it didn't make any difference, that dreaming was part of life, too.

Roz remembered having seen the lights only once, for sure—the night her mother carried her into the living room and set her on the mantel—but how would she have seen them, then? She was in the living room; they were sleeping inside that night, not out. It was the middle of winter.

It struck Roz, as she made her way down to the kitchen, that Mike's house was warmer than it had been for months. The first batch of real spring weather had rolled in. When she got downstairs, Mike wasn't scooping Swiss Miss into mugs for them, didn't have the kettle on to boil the way he usually did. He was just standing on the side porch, and when she walked in, he turned and asked her, "Wanna fish? We could go out and still be back in time for school."

Yes: even in her half-asleep state, she knew she wanted to go. She'd fished once before with Mike, soon after she'd arrived. They'd gone down to the Merrimack River, and after, Mike took her to the Fish Tail Diner for breakfast. This time Mike said they'd try the Artichoke reservoir.

"Put on something warm," he called after her. She was already up the stairs. She dragged out jeans and a sweater from her bureau, pulled them on in a terrible hurry. There was something exciting and slightly forbidden about fishing to Roz, something she'd never done with her mother. Ellie always said there were snakes by the water, and she feared them.

Roz joined Mike outside, in the freshest air, and watched the swallows and a red-winged blackbird diving.

She loved being awake and outside when most other people weren't. She felt expectant, and everything around her seemed slightly magical, possibly dangerous.

The mornings Roz woke up in the tent, after she and Ellie had slept out, were like that. She knew certain things, even before she'd opened her eyes. She could feel whether her mother was beside her in the tent, or whether she had already gone. She never opened her eyes until she was ready for her mother not to be there. Her mother was in the kitchen, she told herself, in the kitchen starting breakfast. Then she rolled onto her stomach and poked her head out the tent flap, looking across the field, at the back of their house. She focused on the house until she could see straight through it, could see her mother standing at the table, pouring juice, or cracking eggs on the side of the mixing bowl. It was on those mornings, after she slept out, that Roz developed her power: to reduce the house to a skeleton of posts and beams, and to find her mother inside it. And when she found her, Roz wanted two things at once: to be exactly where she was, alone in the tent and watching her mother from a distance, and also to be *there*, across the field, in the kitchen right beside her. The need to be with her was always stronger, though, and Roz would pull herself up, run across the wet grass, and burst into the kitchen. Every morning, Ellie Jacoby kissed Roz and held her against her while she rubbed small circles on her back and asked, "Did you dream?"

Mike had never asked, not once. Roz always told him, though, after he got her up from a nightmare, "I can't remember what it was about."

They were barreling along, in the truck. Mike shrugged. "Don't chase it," he told her. "Doesn't matter."

It did matter, though, to Roz. Everything mattered—
she knew that, from her mother—and everything had to
include a dream powerful enough to make her scream.
A scream loud enough to wake up Mike, all the way
across the hall. Her mother had put great stock in dreams.
She believed they were a way that God, or sometimes
the Devil, reached out to people. She believed, Roz remembered now, that they were signs.

"Who do you think it is?" Roz said. "God or the
Devil?"

Mike brought his hand up to his mouth and across the
light stubble on his chin. Mike had a broad face—all the
Jacobys did—and powerful arms. Looking at him, Roz
found it hard to doubt, as she did other times, that Mike
and Ellie were really brother and sister, truly from the
same family. In early morning light, in the cab of Mike's
pickup, it was clear enough that they shared the same
face: open and round, with heavy eyebrows and surprised,
hopeful brown eyes.

"When?"

"In my dreams. God or the Devil reaching out to me?"

"Aw, Roz," he said, flopping his wrist over the steering
wheel. "Don't start on that horseshit." He pushed back
against his seat, as far away from the conversation as he
could get. "You sound like Ellie."

Of course she sounded like Ellie. Who else would she
sound like? "Just pick," she said. "You have to pick one."

The ends of his mouth turned down. "Oh, God," he
finally said, more in exasperation than a real answer.

"Are you sure?" she cried. "But how can you be?"
Faith talk got her heart pumping, as if her mother were
right there in the pickup with them. "When I can't even

remember the dream? How'm I supposed to receive a sign if I can't remember?"

"I didn't say I was sure," Mike answered back, his voice gravelly and tired-sounding. "Unlike your mother, I never claimed to know how it all works. How *any* of it works," he amended.

"So why'd you pick God?"

He sighed again, held up his broad, flat empty palm to her. "Because it's all a goddammed mystery to me," he said. "And isn't God the one who works in mysterious ways?" Mike wasn't going any further with it, Roz could tell. He wanted to fish, not talk. That's why they'd come.

Roz did, too—she wanted to sit on the riverbank, or a rock, and not say a word—just wait with Mike to catch a big one. She couldn't give herself over to things the way Mike could, though. Questions yanked at her, as if her life were one of the stories Mike zapped in and out of when he cruised the tube—missing exact details, not clear how it would turn out. Roz needed the whole story before she could settle into fishing, before she could drop things, or not even bring them up.

What she really wanted was release—as sure and dramatic as the night her mother had set Roz on the mantel. That had been years ago—Roz could tie her shoes, she could write her name, what was she, four? five? Her mother's face was so radiant that in Roz's memory it lit the whole room. A ring of heat pulsed out from the wood stove that dominated their living room, the stovepipe clicking at its hottest. Ellie had her hands around Roz's waist as she hoisted her up and positioned her on the deep mantel that topped their huge fireplace, now cold. She set her on it like a prized possession, like a treasure.

Roz woke up fast because she was afraid, perched so high between the antique candlesticks, and among the stones and the bit of honeycomb her mother had placed there. She pressed her back flat against the wall; she feared toppling off if she leaned forward. Even with her mother's hands around her, the mantel felt too high up.

"Darling," her mother whispered, deep into Roz's ear, "God spoke to me." Pulling back from Roz a little, so that she could look straight at her, Ellie said, "Can you believe it? Can you be*lieve* it? After all this time! I just couldn't hear before. All the anger sealed my ears, sealed my heart against love." Ellie was talking right into Roz's eyes. Her mother was beautiful, Roz thought, and scary.

"I woke up tonight, and knew to go outside, and when I walked out back into the field, I had this wonderful, light feeling. But something was missing, like I'd forgotten to bring something or someone with me."

Roz held her breath and waited for her mother to speak her name. She listened for it with her elephant's ear, her prayer ear, the one that listened and heard loudest and clearest. Her mother did not say Roz's name, though. She said, "I stopped in the middle of the field and turned back to look at the house and try to figure what it was, what I had forgotten to bring with me, and all of a sudden I realized what it was, gone! The hate, Roz! The hate was gone! It slipped out of me, it finally just passed on. That's what woke me up: the evil spirit leaving me. It's gone, it's truly gone, I know that, and I'll never have to carry it again."

Ellie's joy was so big that she took Roz's hands inside her own and clapped them together for her. Roz did not know what Ellie was talking about, but the feeling in the room, radiating out from her mother, was bigger than her words, and the invitation to join in rejoicing was irresistible. Roz's heart was racing, and Ellie wrapped her arms around Roz and said she loved, loved, loved her.

"You are love incarnate, my darling," she told her, pushing Roz's hair away from her face, stroking Roz's cheek with the palm of her hand. "Born of violence, but into love. And love is bigger, so much bigger that it just drowns what came before it, drowns it in love." Ellie hugged Roz again and Roz rubbed small circles on her mother's back.

"You'll know this for yourself, someday," Ellie said. "How forgiveness sets you free."

Roz remembered her mother's words as the sky lightened in imperceptible increments and she watched through the windshield of Mike's truck. They were traveling along the reservoir and the water was glimmering and beautiful. Mike pulled over to park. Roz took the tackle box and pail, and he grabbed the two poles. Descending to the riverbank, Roz dug the heels of her sneakers into the slightly muddy earth.

They settled on a rock, close to the water. Mike handed Roz her pole and she immediately dropped her line in. Mike took a little longer setting himself up. Mike was a big man, and his belly hung over his belt, but he moved with a certain grace. When his line was ready, he flicked his wrist and sent it sailing out across the lake. Then they both settled in, to wait. No one talked.

Mike caught two right away. He reeled them in smooth and steady. The way he did it impressed Roz, how even he was on his end. The first one was small and he threw it back. The next, a bass, he kept.

Roz watched her line, dropped straight down into the dark water. She thought she was on guard for a nibble, but the yank on her line, sudden and strong, amazed her, and she jerked to attention. Mike lullabied her through it: "You've got one now. Pull her in, nice and slow, nice and steady." Roz listened, and became deliberate. She concentrated only on the motion of reeling, the sound of Mike's voice, the effort of steadiness against such resistance. She liked all that. But she did not like the sight she raised up out of the water—the sunfish, thrashing on the end of her own line as if it were crazy, as if it were drowning in air. Drowning would be an awful way to die, worse than falling, worse even than blowing up.

"Keep going," Mike had to tell her. She had stopped.

She reeled the fish up farther, and Mike reached out and took it in his big hand and unhooked it.

"Let it go," Roz urged him. "Let him go."

"Bye, buddy," he said as he held the fish upright and let it slice back into the water. Then he turned and emptied out the bucket that held the bass. "What the hell," he said. "We had a good morning. We gotta get going anyway."

It came as news to Roz—she had forgotten there was something else ahead, as if her day of suspension had itself been suspended. She took the pail and tackle box and reluctantly led the way back to the truck.

She didn't usually like going first. She always thought of Isaac, in the picture from her Bible stories book, walking ahead of Abraham with the long, white beard. Abraham who was going to sacrifice his only son, but Isaac didn't know it yet. Roz could tell, by the picture, that he didn't have an inkling of what his father and God had planned for him. No idea at all. He was even carrying the firewood for his own fire—a little batch of wood strapped to his back. Ellie told Roz that the exact word for that bundle of wood was *faggot*.

It broke Abraham's heart to think of losing his child —*broke* his heart, Ellie always repeated when she read Roz the story—but he was willing to do it because God had asked him to. Roz studied Isaac's face the whole time Ellie read the words, but it never told her a thing. She needed to see his face after, after he understood that he was the sacrifice. How, exactly, did he look then, and what did he think? Where were the words for that? The story Ellie read to Roz wasn't the one she listened for. Ellie told her it was a story about Abraham's willingness to sacrifice. But for Roz it was Isaac's story—Isaac, who didn't suspect what he was up against.

She jerked her head back to check on Mike, lumbering up behind her like a friendly bear. She faced forward again, and smiled, almost as if she had wanted to be scared of Mike, but couldn't be, not of Mike.

Abraham wouldn't really kill Isaac; Roz knew that. God would tell him to sacrifice the ram in the bushes instead. Even so, even knowing how it would turn out, Roz still held her breath every time Abraham bound Isaac and put him on the wood, and every time the ending came as an enormous relief.

Mike said he could swing by Circle Donuts real easy. "Yeah," Roz answered, on cue, "that'd be good." It occurred to Roz, on the way, that her mother could have been wrong about there always being snakes by the water. She hadn't seen a single one.

They decided to eat in for once. She ordered a chocolate cruller with juice, and Mike got two sugars with a large coffee, and they sat in a corner booth. She felt good, she felt as if she had really fished, and as if the fishing had replenished her, so she could keep on, keep after the things she needed to know.

"What's incarnate?" she said.

"What?"

"Incarnate, or something like that." She waved her hand when she said it, all of a sudden self-conscious about not knowing the exact word she was saying. She bit into her cruller.

Mike was squinting from a sip of scalding coffee. "Use it," he told her, "in a sentence."

"Never mind," she said, but something in her pushed ahead anyway. "Love incarnate," she recited. "Mom said it."

Mike stopped chewing. "About what?"

"About me. The night the evil spirit left her."

Mike rolled his eyes.

Roz waited for Mike to say it was horseshit, but he didn't. He rubbed one big hand up and down his face. "Jesus, Roz," he said. "How the hell am I supposed to know? You know how Ellie was when she got going."

Roz dabbed at the glaze sprinkles on the wax tissue with her finger. "You're saying she was crazy."

"Well," he answered her, matter-of-fact, "there are plenty of worse things to be. And it's not like that's *all* she was."

"Yeah," Roz agreed, at home in the larger notion of Ellie.

"Most people are crazy," he said, "to some extent. They have their reasons."

She remembered her mother's words: "Not being listened to makes you crazy." Roz pressed her finger down hard on a crumb. "You mean the rape," she said.

Roz raised her eyes to Mike's face. He was blushing. His face was a deep red, almost a purple.

Mike looked awful. Oh, hadn't they just been fishing? Hadn't they been happy? Her stupid words again, trouble words.

"Ellie talked to you about that?" he said.

"Some," Roz answered him. "Mostly she prayed about it."

"Maybe she should have kept her prayers to herself," Mike said. He looked, disgusted, at his cup of coffee.

Roz kept quiet, but she didn't wish her mother had kept her prayers to herself. She loved the sound of her mother's voice praying, coming through her bedroom wall at night, pulsing like music. The closest she had to it now was hearing the TV downstairs when Mike stayed up late to watch, but the sounds that floated up to her weren't as good. They were fake, she knew—the laughs and the fights, all the sirens, no real fire. Her mother praying was real. Her mother praying was the most real thing Roz knew in the world. It was Roz's own words that caused all the trouble.

Hadn't her words just soured things for Mike? It was written all over him, as if the fish had all wiggled off the hook, as if Roz had erased the whole morning. "Wanna bring home a dozen?" she blurted out. She wasn't through with her cruller, she wasn't even hungry, but it was all she could think to offer him just then, to save the day. It wasn't much—a dozen doughnuts to go—but what else did she have?

"Sure," he said, though she could tell his heart wasn't in it. "You pick." He hoisted up his big body and dug into his pocket to bring up a few loose singles.

In front of the glass display of doughnut trays, she took in all the doughnuts at once, all the frosted, glazed, sprinkled, jellied.

"Can I help you?" The woman behind the counter, a woman with gray hair and cloudy green eyes, was calling to Roz. "Hello there?"

"Oh," Roz said, blushing. "We need a dozen to go."

The woman turned and grabbed a tissue and box, ready to fill Roz's order. Roz began her litany of choice: two glazed, three chocolate, two sprinkles. It sounded like so much to her. She kept thinking that she had used up her twelve, but the woman told her she had more to go. "A coconut, I guess," she continued. She started naming kinds she had never tried, didn't want. She thought about her mother and how she fasted, stopped eating for days at a time. The gray-haired woman kept stacking Roz's choices into the box, waiting for another command, until finally she closed and taped it.

Roz passed the wadded-up dollar bills across the counter. "Sometimes it helps me love," Ellie explained to Roz about her fasting, though Roz could never understand how loving and not eating might be connected. During her fasts, Ellie fixed Roz some of her best breakfasts—blueberry pancakes, scones—and sat with her while she ate them, but she never took a bite, even when Roz offered her one, held out her fork with a chunk of pancake dripping maple syrup. "Not yet, darling," Ellie told her. "I'm still making room for other things I need to know." Needing to know other things: Roz understood about that.

She carried the box back to Mike and set it down. It seemed stupid, again—how little she had to offer him. Mike seemed satisfied, though. He thanked her, and didn't seem as unhappy as before she'd got them. "I'll save some for you," he said.

"Thanks," Roz told him, but even as she answered Mike, she knew that the time was coming for her to fast, too, like her mother, to make room for all the things she needed to know.

At home, she briefly considered starting her fast right away, not even making a lunch for herself, but she couldn't imagine how it would work at school, what she could possibly learn there. She'd have to wait, the way her mother did, until the time was right. She just hoped she'd know, for sure, when that was.

She climbed the stairs to get her backpack. At her bed, she dropped to her knees, yanked down by a force of habit strong enough to have its own gravity. She held her hands tight together, in a fist, and listened for a prayer to come to her.

Nothing came: no prayer, nothing, the way it had been since her mother had gone. *Are you listening, Roz? Listen hard.* She knelt heavy on her knees, as if she were mad at them, and strained to hear anything at all. Finally, though, it was her own small voice that cried out, *From the bottom of my heart.* The same words she had spoken to Scott, when she had forgiven him. Or had he forgiven her? It didn't matter. She knew from her mother how big forgiveness was: so big it washes over everyone.

Roz remembered her mother's prayer, her litany of forgiveness: she forgave the man who put his power over hers. She forgave the people who did not help her when she tried to tell them. She forgave the men and women who threatened to take Roz away from her. Forgiveness was the most important thing in the whole world to Ellie

Jacoby, the thing she told Roz moved people forward, away from the things that bound them, and toward God.

Roz was not moving. The wooden floor ground against her knee bones, and no prayer came to her. All she had for sure was the yearning.

Three

As soon as Roz entered the school, Mr. Renard corralled her with five other students standing near his office door. A few minutes later, he led the little band through the hallway and then down a stairway Roz had never taken before, into the basement of the school—into its hell, she thought, as she walked farther and farther down the slightly darkened hallway, closed doors to the left and right of her. But it didn't feel like hell. It didn't feel like anything yet, just cool and quiet, except for the drone of Mr. Renard's voice.

"Mr. Puccio, who usually handles in-house suspension, is out sick," he was telling them, turning his head around to speak as he continued walking forward. "Ms. Givens, the special-needs teacher, will supervise this week."

Special needs. Roz liked the sound of it. She ran the words inside her head as she continued walking. They were prettier words than saying that she did not have a mother.

Roz couldn't tell by just looking at the other students what their special needs were. Nothing showed on them, any more than Roz's need showed on her. She thought of Isaac's face in her Bible stories book, and how little it told about what his father had planned for him.

At the farthest end of the hallway, Mr. Renard herded them into a regular, stuffy classroom, with uneven rows of desks, one wall of small windows high up, reaching for the ground-level light. "Take a seat," he directed them. "Ms. Givens will be here in just a minute. And let me make it clear right now that if there are any problems," and then he paused, for emphasis, "you will answer to me."

I am answerable to no man. Roz almost said it out loud. *Only to God.* They were her mother's words, the ones she spoke to the policeman peering in at them through the screen door. He'd come to deliver the court order demanding that Ellie enroll Roz in an accredited school. Ellie dropped the hook into the eye and latched the door against him. Roz remembered her mother's low, scary whisper.

"Are we understood?" Mr. Renard drew in his chin and raised his eyebrows.

The weak chorus of yeses apparently satisfied Mr. Renard, because he told them, "All right, then," and left the room.

The only other girl in their group sat heavy and sullen-looking next to Roz. The name on her loose-leaf binder, in hot-pink colored-in letters, read "Angela Gilbert." Roz wondered what had suspended her, what about her could not be tolerated. She didn't look evil to Roz, just miserable.

"Why don't you make a video, you're so interested?" Angela leaned close to Roz's face to say it.

Roz pulled back. She had been staring unabashedly, as if she were invisible, or a baby, and could get away with it. She immediately looked away. She told Angela, though, "I was wondering what you did to get here."

"Here?" she said. Angela didn't sound mad anymore. "Suspended? I called Mrs. Overholder a fucking bitch."

The boys, who had been talking among themselves behind them, laughed when she said it. One, a boy with red hair, said, "All *right*."

Words, then. Their words suspended them, words without FIRE: Facts, Incidents, Reasons, Examples. Roz thought about the words that had spoiled Mike's morning—*incarnate, evil spirit, rape*—and about the words people had for her mother—*crazy, hero*—words that didn't begin to tell the whole story.

And then Ms. Givens arrived, and words were practically the first thing she asked for. She breezed into the classroom—a sparky woman with curly hair, dressed in a long yellow skirt and close-cropped black shirt, a bumblebee, Roz thought—and introduced herself. "For those of you who don't already know me," she said, making big eyes at the boys in the back, who obviously knew her well, "I'm Ms. Givens." She said "Ms." like "Mizzz." She had a wonderful smile. She didn't look like a punishment to Roz.

But then she asked them to spread out to desks around the room, so that they could have space and quiet in which to do their work, and handed out sheets of white, lined paper, and said to them, "Would you please write the story of why you are here today."

The exploding sound erupted in Roz. A story about the story that got her in trouble? She held perfectly still, and tried to drown everything inside her. One boy asked how long it had to be. Another boy asked if spelling counted. Ms. Givens shook her head and said, "Just tell me your story."

Where would Roz's words land her this time? In the basement of the basement? There seemed no end to anything. The day loomed in front of her, pouring into the week and then all the weeks and years of school to come, a taste of eternity.

The urge to call Nate came over her in a wave, so strong that she tightened her hands around the edges of her desk just to keep herself seated. Just to hear him breathe. No words at all. She'd call him after school, she promised herself. But she had called him yesterday. Yesterday? Then the call hadn't lasted her even a day. Things were running out on her faster than ever.

She knew that she was losing ground. Things weren't getting more settled, they were getting less settled. Things were building up. She could feel it, the way she'd felt her mother leaving, a long time before Ellie ever disappeared off the mountain. Almost as if she were swimming away, slicing through the water with powerful, silent strokes. Roz could not have said so in words. And it would have been impossible to prove—losing someone even as you're standing at a table with her, listening to a Bible story, baking bread.

But toward the end, her mother was always gone from the tent no matter how early Roz made herself wake up, and when she X-rayed the back of their house with the sheer force of her vision, burned through the clapboards to the posts and beams, it took Roz longer and longer to find her mother. What she saw, first, was an empty kitchen, the mixing bowls nesting inside one another on the shelf, no fire in the stove.

Angela wanted to know if the story counted for their final grade, and one boy kept asking, "What about swears? What if there are swears in our story?" but Ms. Givens brushed away their questions like little bugs and said, "Begin when you're ready," as if the only thing that really mattered was the story itself. And that scared Roz, because she felt the same way, and she didn't have the story.

One by one, the others set to writing. Roz could feel Angela go away from her, into the words that were spilling across her paper. Roz hadn't even lifted her pen.

Ms. Givens came and stood beside Roz. Roz felt her breath, warm and gentle enough to melt her. She bent in closer to her desk, as if an invisible weight were pressing her forward, and closed her eyes. She saw her mother hauling water. Their pipes had frozen and she and her mother hauled water from the brook up to the house, water for drinking and cooking and pouring into the toilet to make it flush. Ellie had found an old wooden yoke in the barn, and she put it across her shoulders, and used it to carry two big black buckets that she hooked on each end of the yoke. Roz traipsed behind her mother, toting a big plastic jug herself, and watched her mother's body, her arms spread out along the bar of the yoke as if she were on a cross, step by step hauling all that heavy water to the house.

Ms. Givens had crouched down so her head was close. "Roz," she whispered, "I can't let you sit idle the whole time."

Idle. Roz saw their old pickup truck, exhaling clouds of exhaust into the winter morning. Her mother warmed it up on days she delivered her bread to the stores in town, and Roz watched it from the kitchen, listened to it race until her mother stomped on the accelerator pedal to calm it down. It sounded so frenzied, put out such billows of smoke, but the heap of rusting gray metal just sat there. All show, no go. Idling.

Roz opened her eyes and picked up her pen. She felt Ms. Givens move on, a blur of yellow and black in Roz's peripheral vision. Across the center of her page she drew the yoke and the two buckets hanging from it. Then she began on her mother's figure, from the back, walking away from the water, all in black ballpoint pen, no real colors. After she finished her picture, she considered words she could be sure of, beyond doubt. Finally, at the bottom of her paper, she wrote her mother's name: Ellen Burns Jacoby. She tried to make the letters sparse and elegant, the way they read on her favorite tombstones, not the round, fat letters on Angela Gilbert's binder. She worked a long time on them, and when she was finished, she walked up and put it on Ms. Givens's desk, as the others had already done. On the way back to her seat, she felt, for just a second, the suspended sensation she had hoped for, the one that came on the bridge she crossed with her mother.

Ms. Givens called her back before Roz had even sat down. As Roz approached her, she leaned in to Roz across her desk, and whispered, "This is beautiful! I love it! What a great start!"

They filled the rest of the morning with worksheet papers for math and social studies, but that afternoon, Ms. Givens let them write more. "This time," she told them, "I want you to tell me your story, but I want you to change it somehow. Change the names, if you want. Change how it happened. The ending. The beginning. Whatever you want—as long as you still believe it, this changed version. One thing you might ask yourself, if you get stuck, is 'What could happen next?' "

Roz started her second drawing exactly as she had her first one, as if there were really no choice: the yoke, and the same black buckets hanging from each end. This time, though, she didn't sketch in any figure at all: this time it was just the yoke and buckets and a pool of water. Her mother was gone, and drawing that, even though it was less, took her longer. When Ms. Givens announced that it was time to stop, Roz reluctantly turned in her paper, and said, "I'm not done." Ms. Givens smiled and answered, "Of course you're not. We'll give it more time tomorrow."

When Roz got home, Mike was working at the bench. "Another day in the salt mines?"

"Yeah," she said, but then qualified: "Better than usual." She was still thinking about her picture, seeing it in color, the entire page a deep blue for the water, and the black buckets on either side of the yoke, like eyes.

That night in bed, she pictured Ms. Givens in her yellow and black, brushing away questions until there was only quiet. What could happen next, Roz asked herself. Just as she was falling asleep, she remembered that she had forgotten to call Nate, and it pleased her, made her feel as if she had an extra one due her, somehow, for having wanted to call so badly and then not done it.

———

On Wednesday, Ms. Givens wore flowers, reds and oranges and pinks all over her dress. She told the class, which had gained another four students, that they could write, or tell, any story they wanted to. She put a stack of clean paper on her desk for everyone to use as they needed, and when Roz came up to her desk, she carefully pulled out Roz's drawings from her cloth book bag. She had put them inside plastic sleeves. It startled Roz to see them like that—protected, handled so carefully. It seemed that whatever Ms. Givens was giving back was more important than what Roz had turned in. It scared her a little. She took them from Ms. Givens and walked back to her desk. The plastic covers caught the sunlight and Roz couldn't see the pictures clearly until she pulled them out of their protectors. From behind her, Roz heard Angela's voice, talking to no one in particular, "She didn't say we could do cartoons."

Oh, God. Roz looked down at what she had made, and they weren't anything like she remembered or hoped—no color, no perfect shapes. Just stupid, awkward, ballpoint-pen drawings, with pale blue lines streaking across them. They looked to Roz as if a little baby had done them. Ellie's hands were spiders, her shoulders were ridiculously wide. Where was the pool of blue? She turned them face down on her desk, and sat still. What did they have to do with anything anyway?

Ms. Givens was making her way around the classroom. She moved from desk to desk, toting a plastic milk crate with her, which she sat on while she talked to each person privately. When she got to Roz she said, "Any new ideas?" Roz shook her head. It was funny: she wanted Ms. Givens to stay right where she was, perched on the red milk crate beside her, but she couldn't get her mouth to open, to form any words at all to keep her there. When Roz didn't say anything, Ms. Givens just sat for a minute and then said, "Give it time," and moved on.

It was all Roz could do not to reach out and grab her dress as she walked away, yank her back to where she'd been beside her, tell her just to stay put and not say a single word. Roz hated this stupid class. She picked up her pencil and started scratching across the page—a long and narrow box.

It was the mantel, the night her mother had set her on top of it. Roz could see that now, and she began drawing Ellie's treasures on top of it: the old brass candlesticks and the piece of honeycomb, and, on the right-hand side, the arrangement of stones they had collected on their walks. As she drew them, she remembered how smooth the stones had felt against the palm of her hand, how pleasing it had been to hold them, and she drew several more, more than had actually been there, for the pleasure of making the shapes and remembering how they had felt.

She left her own figure till last, though she'd saved room for it, on the mantel, between the candlesticks. Finally, when everything else was in place, she began to pencil herself in.

Her first sketch was impossible—she made herself big and stupid-looking, oversized, next to the objects that had turned out so well. There wasn't even room for her whole body on the page, her head went right off the top of the paper. It looked crazy to her. Had she dreamed it, dreamed the whole thing? She erased and tried again, to work herself into her picture, but this time she looked like Humpty Dumpty about to topple, round and freakish. She gouged her portrait with pink streaks from her eraser, made the bottom part of the paper moist from holding it down with her sweaty hand while she tried to make the messed-up part clean again. She rubbed so hard that a small hole appeared in the paper where she had been trying to put her figure, and when she saw what she had done, what a big fat mess she had made of it, she crumpled the whole sheet and threw it hard at the wastebasket. It went straight in, a clean shot.

Ms. Givens, who was leaning in to the boy with red hair who had asked about swears, looked at Roz for just a moment and then went back to her conference. Roz folded her arms and slumped down in her seat. After a few minutes, Ms. Givens made her way over to Roz.

Roz sunk lower in her seat. To her horror, she realized that she was close to crying. She felt the tears in her throat, coming up fast, and she felt powerless to stop them. She coughed, and tapped on her desk top with her closed fist.

No one said anything, but there was a lot somebody wasn't saying. All Ms. Givens finally told her, bending down so that she was even with Roz, face-to-face, was "Please don't give up."

Roz slid her arms over her desk, and laid her head down on them and closed her eyes. She kept her eyes closed tight, and felt how much it hurt, how much it stabbed in the back of the throat, not to cry.

A while later—Roz couldn't tell if it was much later, or just a few minutes—she heard Ms. Givens tell everyone "to begin to stop." They would gather in the back of the room, and anyone who wanted to share his or her story could do that. No one had to read who didn't want to.

"Roz?" Ms. Givens's voice was faraway-sounding because Roz's head was so nestled into her arms and the cocoon of her own breath. "Will you join us?"

Roz pulled her head up and blinked.

"We wouldn't want to begin without you," Ms. Givens said, extending her arm from where she sat in the back of the classroom, as if Roz could reach out and take her hand to help her rise. Roz slowly stood and then made her way back to the others, and sat down Indian-style on the floor.

Ms. Givens turned to Angela, in the author's chair, and said, "We're all ears."

Angela squirmed in the seat and began. She read fast and very quietly, running all her words together—a different voice from the one she used to talk to Roz. *SometimesIdon'tlovemymothershetakesme—*

Ms. Givens jumped in and begged her to slow down and read so everyone could hear her. "It's so good," she said, "let everyone hear it."

Angela started again: *Sometimes I don't love my mother.*

Roz, who had been inspecting the heels of her shoes, lifted her head and stared at Angela. Angela was round, with coiled blond curls. Her hair looked wired to Roz, about to spring. Had she said she did not love her mother? Or did Roz dream that? Had she slept, was she still sleeping? Roz studied Angela's face to see if it told anything, but it didn't.

Angela was reading fast again, the words tumbling out as she told about the time her mother grounded her for no good reason at all. She was in such a hurry to get to the end that she tripped over two words in the last sentence and had to go back to the beginning to have it make any sense at all. As soon as she finished, she kicked out her legs and then looped them on either leg of the chair.

Ms. Givens thanked Angela for reading and asked if there were questions or comments. Almost everyone's hand shot up.

"You don't love your mother?" Roz said. She had not raised her hand.

Angela had been surveying the waving arms in front of her, weighing who she would call on first. "What?" she said to Roz.

"You don't love your mother," Roz said again, not a question this time.

Ms. Givens started to remind Roz to raise her hand if she had something to say, but Angela's eruption cut her off. "*Sometimes,*" Angela shot back at Roz. "I said *sometimes.*" She held up her paper and jabbed her finger across the first line. "*Sometimes* I don't love my mother. *Sometimes.* See? Don't you even listen?"

Roz just watched Angela, and finally said, "How could you say that?" She was practically whispering.

Everyone started to talk at once. Ms. Givens announced that Angela was the author and would answer the questions, and Angela was talking faster than ever, but Roz was not listening, because she had heard what she had heard: that Angela did not love her mother. *Sometimes*—she remembered Angela's lips mouthing that word, but Roz was forgetting it faster than she was remembering it. Her listening had become rain, washing away each word as it was spoken.

What could happen if you didn't love your mother? What could happen next? Anything could happen. You could kill your mother, you could find her on a mountain and push her right over the edge. You could watch her fall and then sneak back home and wait in the empty kitchen for someone to come and tell you what you already know better than anyone in the world: that your mother is gone.

She would have hit Angela if she thought it would do any good—but her hands remembered. Instead, she sat on them while things—Angela talking, the day, other kids reading their stories—went on without her. She thought about Nate, and how she would call him, about how it had been two days. She could feel her fingers pushing the buttons.

A little bit before three, at the phone booth on High Street, near the intersection with State, she pressed in Nate's phone number, so much a part of her memory that it was like breath, or her own name, and waited while her call made its way to New Jersey. Just knowing that it was going through calmed her. But it didn't go through: instead, she heard a different kind of ringing, as if the call had been transferred, and then the robot voice of a recording. "The number you have reached . . ." She must have misdialed, she told herself, but the voice was repeating, in its dead, toneless way, the exact number she wanted. ". . . has been changed." No. She slammed the receiver down and pulled it tight against its holder. No. Her money poured back into the cup. She yanked the receiver up and force-fed her coins and jabbed the silver buttons. Again she could not get through. The same dead voice came on to tell her that the number she had reached had been changed. The new number, the voice continued—and Roz's heart soared, for just an instant—was unlisted, at the customer's request.

Roz moaned out loud. She wanted to scream, to howl,

to explode into the sky and fall down on people in little tiny pieces of herself. Roz had to have Nate Thompson's voice in her life the way she had to have air. Nate was all that was left of her mother, the person she had died for.

What was happening, she asked herself. Not what could happen next, but what was happening right now, this very second that she was asking, because things felt like they were falling down around her, on top of her. How did people disconnect? How did someone just disconnect? Poof. Gone.

She returned the receiver to its cradle for the final time and turned away. Without thinking, she headed toward home, following the same route she always took, never even looking up. No heron swooped down over her head, no family of foxes crossed the road in front of her, but as she walked it just slid inside her, smooth as a swimmer's stroke, that the unlisted number was surely a sign. As sure as thunder in a snowstorm, a sign to go and find Nate, and see for herself, to get the story straight. As soon as she saw it, it was obvious.

And not just a sign but a warning, too—an urgent warning: his voice had already disconnected, he had joined the unlisted of Montclair, New Jersey; he, too, was swimming away from her, she could feel it. She had to get her hands on him soon, like doubting Thomas, like Mike holding the soldiers with holes in their chests. To find out for herself, once and for all, what had happened. The force of the realization reverberated all through her, as she cut across their scruffy lawn and pushed open the front door.

Mike was on the phone, looking as if all he wanted to

do was to get off it. He motioned her ahead into the kitchen. Roz sat down at the table, to think. She could hear the working innards of the old electric clock over her head, whenever the big black hands moved.

A minute later, Mike came in, rubbing the back of his neck. He looked at her for a second without speaking. "There're doughnuts," he finally said. "You hungry?"

No sooner had he asked than she knew it was time to begin her fast. Things were coming to her quickly now: knowing, for sure, what to do. "That's okay," she said.

"There's glazed left," he said. "Go ahead."

Roz shook her head. "No thanks."

"Well, why the hell not?" he said, as if he were mad, as if it mattered.

Roz sat up in her chair, her eyes bigger. Did she have to tell him why? He'd only think it was horseshit. "I'm not hungry," she said, and blushed for her lie.

"Since when?" He leaned one hand against the counter. "What, you're sick of glazed?" he said. "It's not like that's the only kind left," he told her, picking up the box and holding it out to her. "You picked 'em out yourself, for Christsake."

Roz looked down.

"They have like fifty varieties, Roz. You have your cinnamon, your jellies, your sprinkles." He was talking louder than he needed to for Roz to hear him. "Muffins," he finished. He shook the box a little. "My point is, Roz, you could tell me, if there's a problem."

It made Roz want to throw up, what was happening between Mike and her, the feeling in the kitchen between them. "I'm sorry," she said. She didn't even need to say it: from the bottom of my heart. She wanted to take the entire box of doughnuts and eat every last one. This wasn't how fasting was supposed to work. Where was the love, where were the things she didn't know?

Mike turned and tossed the box back on the counter. "They want us to go for family counseling," he said.

Roz looked at his big back, the sloping shoulders.

"That teacher of yours at school, she recommended we see a counselor," he said. "That was the school, they just called." He turned and gave her a resigned, a sorry smile.

"What is it?" she asked him, dreading. She could tell, by the way he'd said it, that it was bad. "Family counseling."

"Oh, your basic tell-me-about-it crap," he said. "Talk. More talk. I don't know." He shrugged. He looked miserable to Roz, big and tired. He grabbed the box of doughnuts, put it on the table between them, and sat down in the chair opposite her.

Roz thought of anything she could say, any offering for the trouble she caused. Finally she fed him his own words of comfort: "It'll blow over." She saw the funnel of wind coming.

"Yeah," he said, and opened the box and pulled out a jelly. "Go ahead." He nodded at her, and she took the coconut.

Four

Ellie Jacoby had always told her daughter, "When you are doing right, a power comes into you," and after Roz saw clearly what she was meant to do, she did feel a power inside her, as if she were wired to an arrow soon to be sprung into motion, set on its course, a perfect arc. Even school became tolerable, even the upcoming family counseling. Roz took them in stride, because in her heart she had moved on to a plan that was bigger than day-to-day, a plan that took into account all the things she needed to know.

On the afternoon of their appointment ten days later, Mike took Roz to McDonald's for an early dinner. Roz knew he was trying to make the best of a bad situation. There was a cold spring rain coming down, and they ate in the cab of Mike's pickup, with the heater turned on full blast. Her shake was so thick she could barely suck it up through the straw.

"How should we do this?" Roz wanted to know. They hadn't talked about it at all since that first day.

"Beats me," he said. Then he followed up right away with, "For Christsake don't get started on dreams. They go nuts over that stuff. We'll be there all night." He bit deep into his Quarter Pounder.

"How can I tell what I don't even remember?"

"That's the shit they love the most," he said.

"But if you can't remember it—" she started, but he cut her off.

"Look, Roz," Mike said. "I don't claim to know how it works. They just go digging for things, picking at scabs until you bleed all over again. I had enough at the V.A. hospital."

"Okay," Roz said, not exactly sure what she was agreeing to, but willing.

"I get the feeling they just want to be sure that you know how Ellie really died," he said. He shot her a look as he tilted his head back to catch some of the ice at the bottom of his cup. "You know," he said, "how she act-u-ally died. Otherwise these sessions might go on and on."

Roz was gobbling french fries, one after the other, and didn't answer. "So if you could do that," Mike continued, "just let them know that you know, it might ex-pe-dite matters, if you know what I mean."

Roz could do that. She could certainly tell them the little bit that she knew, the puny words she'd been given: *boy, mountain, fall.* What she had to offer wasn't enough, though—not if, like her, they wanted the details, the whole story. "You sure that's what they're after?" she asked.

"As far as I can make out," he told her. And having

said what he had to say, he began stuffing all the garbage, the cups and containers, the wad of unused napkins and the straw wrappers, back into the bag. He pitched it into the can from his rolled-down window, and then pulled the truck out of the lot, thumping his thumbs against the steering wheel and putting on a little speed.

The therapist greeted him in the waiting room, just as Mike was opening an old issue of *Life* magazine. He extended his hand to them right away, first to Roz, then to Mike. "I'm Frank Kerchaw," he said. Shaking hands always embarrassed Roz, but there was no way around it, and so she put her hand in his, and it was warm and strong, and she was sorry for a second that she hadn't put any spunk into her own shake. She noticed that Mike seemed uncomfortable, too. He stood with his feet wide apart, as if he were planting them, and answered in a voice Roz didn't recognize when he said, "Mike Jacoby," back to Frank.

Frank motioned them down the hall to his office and Roz and Mike marched single file, Roz in front, into the room. It felt like school to Roz, like going to Mr. Renard's office, or going to sit on the bench. There was even the faint smell of french fries, the way the school cafeteria smelled, but she realized that it came from Mike and her, not the office. There was a small puffy couch in it and two director's chairs and another chair upholstered in dark blue and purple stripes that Roz somehow knew was Frank Kerchaw's place.

Roz and Mike dropped down next to each other on the puffy couch, and Frank sat directly opposite them. He was talking to Mike about something. Roz didn't listen; she knew they weren't saying anything that mattered yet. She could tell by the way Mike was nodding

—the same way he did when people dropped off something to be fixed, before they actually handed over the busted toaster or vacuum cleaner and he could check for himself just what was wrong. She looked around at the things in the room: a box of tissues, some painted eggs on the table beside her, and a little metal sculpture of two people on a wire seesaw. She wanted to lean over and set it in motion, to see if it really worked, but she didn't dare. The posters on the wall showed opening flowers. She could see vacuum tracks on the carpet; everything was clean.

Now things were starting. It was quiet. Frank was looking at her and Mike was looking down. Someone must have said something to her and she hadn't heard.

"I was just asking how long you'd been in Newburyport, Roz," Frank said.

So it still wasn't anything. Roz told him, "Since the fall."

Frank leaned forward in his chair a little bit. He was tall, with dark wiry hair, and when he leaned toward them his pants pulled up and Roz could see that his socks went up high, higher than Mike's did, so that none of his skin showed at all.

"Mr. Renard filled me in a little bit about what's been happening at school, Roz. But I'd like to hear from you, and then from you, Mike, about how you see things, what you might see as a problem." He looked first at Roz and then at Mike, and then there was silence.

Mike cleared his throat and shifted on the couch. It wasn't really big enough for him. When he moved he set off motion all through the cushions, like a motorboat going by on a lake, rocking the farthest canoe. Roz was the canoe.

"Things are okay," Mike started. His voice sounded funny to Roz, still not his own. "I'd say things are going along pretty well, all things considered," Mike said, and he looked to Roz—her turn.

"Yeah," Roz said. "They're all right." She wasn't sure what they were talking about.

Frank said that Mr. Renard had said there'd been some problems at school.

Roz nodded.

"There is a problem?"

"I guess," Roz said.

"And what is it?" Frank asked.

"My mother died," Roz told him. Was that what he was asking?

Frank nodded and said that he was sorry.

Roz told him, "It's not your fault." She felt Mike shifting again, but she didn't look at him. She reminded herself not to mention any dreams.

Frank asked her whose fault it was.

"That my mother died?" Was something wrong with Frank? Didn't he know anything? "No one's," she said. "It wasn't anybody's fault. God called her."

Frank nodded again and turned to Mike. "Roz's mother was your sister, is that right, Mike?"

Mike looked startled to be addressed. "Oh, yeah," he answered. "Ellie was my sister, that's right."

"So you've both lost someone close to you," Frank continued, "and that's hard, and there have been a lot of changes."

"That's for sure," Mike said right back at him, and Roz felt herself breathe for the first time, as if something was all right. Mike sounded like Mike again.

"How did your mother die, Roz?" Frank asked next.

It hadn't taken him long to get there, just as Mike had warned her, but she was ready for him. It was no different from Scott's voice calling out, "*Who* got blasted?" But this time she was prepared.

"She fell," Roz answered him. "She fell off a mountain when she was trying to save a boy who was lost. She's a heroine," she finished.

"Was she alone?" Frank asked.

"What?"

"When she fell," he said. "Was she alone when she fell off the mountain?"

Why was he still talking about it? Why were his lips still moving? She had given him the answer. There wasn't any more. How could anyone know unless they were there? Other people didn't know. Nate knew. So did her mother, but she was gone. Isaac knew, but no one ever told his side of the story.

A tune pushed into her head and she started to hum, very softly at first, and then louder as she tried to remember what it was, where it came from. What was the name of the song? If she hummed the whole thing through to the end, she would remember.

"Roz?"

She had to start over. If she got interrupted she had to start over, or she would never remember it. She started in again.

Roz's mother sang to her sometimes, made up her own songs when she put Roz to bed, or when she worked in the garden, or when they took walks together. They were always about what was happening right then: the bushes on either side of them with lit-tle roses, lit-tle roses, or the earthworm in the earth, in the earth. Just whatever was around them, any little thing that her mother found to put in the song, so that there were never two songs exactly alike.

Mike nudged her with his elbow. "Quit it, Roz," he said, and she did. The tune went right out of her head.

Frank changed the subject. He asked Roz about school and what classes she liked, and then he asked Mike questions that Roz didn't listen to or care about. Dreams never came up. After a while, Frank asked each of them what they would like to have happen, if there was any change they would like to see in how things were going at school. Mike shrugged as if he didn't know, but started talking right away. "School's tough," he said. "A lot of bullshit to cut through, and you more or less just have to get it over with, you know?"

Frank asked Roz what she wanted.

She wanted the truth. She wanted to know what happened, but how could Frank help her with that? He wasn't there. Maybe she wanted to know what she dreamed at night. But she wouldn't mention dreams for anything, not after what Mike had told her. They'd be there all night. There wasn't enough room; they'd have to sleep sitting up. And Frank would watch her sleep, see her fall inside her dream. What would he be able to see? What shows of a dream? Mike was right to say steer clear. But what else could she tell Frank she wanted?

"A miracle," she answered. Even just to say the word felt good to her.

"A miracle," Frank repeated. Roz could feel Mike's disappointment next to her. She hadn't said anything about the dreams, but it was as if she had, the sinking inside him that she felt all through her. She had stumbled into horseshit again.

"What kind of miracle?" Frank asked her. She looked

at Mike, but his hands were folded and he was staring down at them.

What kind? She couldn't say. Planning out exactly what she wanted ran contrary to how miracles worked. She knew from her mother: don't ask for anything; just offer up what you have and open your heart to God's response. Big things can happen. Big changes. Glorious changes.

Frank was waiting for her. She hadn't bothered to speak any of the thoughts that had gone through her mind. "Where were we?" Roz asked.

"I had asked what kind of miracle."

"Better not to say," she managed to get out.

"Then could you tell me what a miracle is, how it works?"

"You don't know?" Roz asked him. It seemed hard to believe, how a man like that could not know, sitting in his office, in his blue-and-purple-striped chair.

"Well," Frank said, "people have different ideas about what things are and what they mean. I have my own ideas, but right now I'm more interested in hearing what you think about it."

Roz was feeling a little nervous about leaving Mike behind. "It's horseshit," she said, by way of including him. She looked over at him again, to see if she'd fixed things, but his face was red, his neck, too.

"To talk about it, I mean," she added. And just then she could see Mike's point: it wasn't any good, trying to talk to other people about these things. They never came out right, they never set the room on fire the way her mother's stories did. Roz's words just made trouble. "Forget it," she said. She thought that forgetting it was the best way to go just then. Roz felt tired, the way she did in the kitchen after a nightmare, when she needed to go back to sleep. Was it over, she wondered. Who got to say when it was over?

"I want to thank you both for talking with me," Frank told them. He was finishing up, though Roz didn't get that at first. "I enjoyed meeting you."

"Right, right," Mike said, pushing his big frame off the puffy couch.

They walked out of the office side by side. "That's over," Mike whispered to her as soon as they reached the waiting room. "Now you can sing."

She could feel them both forgetting everything, shedding their hour with Frank and letting it roll away behind them, across the parking lot, as they walked to the truck and headed home.

The next day, as if to draw her back to her bigger plan, Roz received another sign. Everything was telling her something! This sign came from a completely unexpected source: her own body. She felt it happening first during chorus—a wet, dropping-down feeling, as if she were separating from herself along some interior seam. She thought that something else had gone wrong, another disconnection, and all she could think to do was carry on, resigned to unknown damage. On her way home, though, out of the blue, it hit her, exactly what it was: her own blood pouring out of her.

She walked straight into the house and climbed the stairs to the bathroom. She pulled off her sweater, kicked off her sneakers, yanked at her socks, unzipped and pulled down her jeans and stained underpants. She stepped out of them and left all the clothes in a heap on the floor and then leaned in close to the mirror over the sink, looking at her reflection for confirmation of something she already knew. But she did not look different, not the slightest bit. She just *was* different, changed.

Roz ran the water until it was hot, soaked a washcloth in it, and then washed the dried blood from the insides of her thighs, tenderly cleaning herself, the way her mother had dabbed around Roz's cuts when she was a child.

She thought it was funny, how she'd worried that she'd been given a sign but missed it. There was no missing your own blood! And how she'd assumed that signs always came from outside: the air, the sky, the woods—and here was this clear and true thing right inside her. She wished she could tell her mother that part—about it being inside her the whole time.

Roz reached under the sink and pulled out the box of pads. Ellie had given it to her over a year ago, and Roz had brought the box with her to Newburyport and stored it under the sink for when the time came. Ellie had explained all about menstruation to Roz. She talked about body things a lot. She told Roz, every month, when she felt her own period coming on. She said she could feel it building up inside her, a pressure. Roz had assumed that she would feel it building up inside her, too, but she hadn't. She felt so surprised, even though it was something she'd known was coming.

Naked, Roz tiptoed down the hall and into her bedroom, grabbed clean underpants from her dresser, and sprinted back to the bathroom. She unfolded a pad and laid it inside her underpants, pressing the sticky backing against the cloth before she stepped into them and pulled them up. She completely dressed herself again. Why had she taken off all her clothes in the first place? She didn't know.

She checked her reflection one more time, in the mirror, looking for any difference that might show, but none did. Everything, though, had changed. She walked into her bedroom and dropped to her knees by the bed.

She thought she wanted to give thanks. But it wasn't gratitude that flooded her; it was dread. She felt more clearly than ever that it was time to act, and more than anything in the world she wanted the clarity to pass from her. She wanted it to rise above her and float away, another cloud she could watch sail overhead in the graveyard. But her mission sat immovable within her, like a stone, like a boulder that could not be pushed aside, not even by dread or fear. She remembered when her mother settled on something being right—a conviction, a plan —the silence and the stubbornness that seeped through the whole house, a muscle tightening on itself. "Under siege"—that's what her mother had told her about their fight with the schools. They were under siege from the authorities, and she would fight unto death if she had to, because there was no compromising the truth. "We stand to lose everything," her mother had told her one night, clearly willing to pay the price. "Even each other."

Roz wished she had her mother's sureness, wished she had God's voice in her ear. A person would surely answer God. But Roz didn't fool herself that it was God calling her to go to Montclair and see Nate Thompson with her very own eyes. It was her own self calling, and she had to answer all the same.

A picture from Roz's Bible stories book appeared behind her closed eyes, then: the picture of Jesus leaning against a rock, praying. Roz remembered him crying, but could that be right? Did Jesus cry? Or was it sweat, big cartoon drops running down his face? He was filled with dread because he knew what was going to happen to him: he was going to die. His friends were going to betray him and he was going to be crucified. Jesus begged to have it not happen, to "let this cup pass" from him, but it was going to happen anyway.

Roz did not know what would happen to her, did not know what was waiting for her, in her cup. It could be anything. Anything could happen, she could die. Anyone could die, anytime. She could certainly die. Was she sure, absolutely sure, that she had to go and find Nate? Did it really matter, what was real?

This was no prayer she was saying. She lifted herself up off her knees and flopped onto the bed. Roz lay across her sagging mattress and looked down at the wide pine floorboards, separated from one another by distant grooves that collected dust and dirt and any little thing that ended up on the sloping floor.

She stayed there for a long time, finally rolled over onto her back and lay studying the hairline cracks that streaked through her ceiling. She did need to know the truth, and after that, to believe it: her hands right on the wound, the same as Thomas, and Mike, and the TV. She was scared, but willing, and it was the willingness that finally pulled her back inside the day. She lifted herself off the bed and went downstairs to see what Mike was making for dinner. She promised herself, though, that she'd go to Montclair and find Nate for herself. Even if it cost her everything.

Five

"I want to get to Montclair, New Jersey," she told the person who answered the phone. She had dialed the number listed under BUS LINES in the yellow pages. Roz was calling from the same phone on High Street, near the World War I cannon, not far from the statue of George Washington, that she had always used to call Nate. It was business that had no place in Mike's house, on his line.

"From where?" the woman asked her.

"From here," Roz answered.

The woman sighed, as if Roz had told a joke the woman was tired of hearing. "Where's here?"

"Oh," Roz said. What did she want to know? The street? The exact location of the phone booth? Would the bus come pick her up right there?

"What city?" the woman spat out.

"Oh," Roz said again, "oh. Newburyport." There was a pause, and then, as if the woman had been waiting all day to pour out the information, she started rattling off days and times and switches in Boston and New York. Roz was unprepared for the assault. She was not even holding a pen, she had no paper in front of her. She listened, frozen, to the woman's recitation—"excluding Sundays and holidays," "transfer point"—and then dry-whispered thank you and hung up. She was shaking. She had told herself: one thing a day, one day at a time, until finally all the things would be done and she would go. It was, to Roz, the same as baking: standing with her mother at the wooden table, adding one ingredient at a time. A cup of flour, and then another cup of flour, and then another, adding and kneading, until they had dough. Every golden-crusted loaf she pulled out from the oven really was a miracle to her, because she knew for a fact the simple ingredients that had created it.

She had thought she could make her trip the same way, bit by simple bit. And now Roz had done her first thing, added the first cup of flour, but she held nothing in her hand. She stared at the receiver hanging in its silver cradle.

Tomorrow: she would call back tomorrow and ask again. Sweet relief started to pump all through her. Maybe someone different would answer the phone. And even if it was the same woman, she might not remember that Roz had called before, and even if she did, she wouldn't be able to see Roz.

The next day after school, same time, same place, she called back. First she was put on hold, and then a man answered. She was ready for him. "I need to go to Mont-clair, New Jersey, from Newburyport, Massachusetts," she said. It was sounding neater, more possible. This man went much slower. She had her pen ready, and she wrote down everything he told her. He said she would have to switch buses in Boston and New York. She wrote all the words down and did not begin to think about what they meant until she had thanked him and hung up.

He had told her the round-trip fare would cost around sixty dollars. He couldn't give an exact figure because she'd use a different bus line from New York to Montclair, and he didn't know its prices. "But sixty dollars should do it for you," he'd said. She stared down at the number she had gouged into the paper—more than fifty dollars to get her to Nate and bring her back home again. She shoved the paper in her pocket and started walking.

She thought about where money came from. From Mike's pockets—crumpled dollar bills that he stuck into his jeans pockets and pulled out as he needed them. From the government check he got sent every month, for whatever he'd done in Vietnam. From the junk drawer in the kitchen where Mike kept bread and milk money—none of it hers. Where else? From fixing things, about which she knew nothing. From selling things.

That night, Roz lay in bed and made a mental inventory of everything she owned that she thought might be of value. She started with her mother's ashes—in a box in her closet. She saw into the closet, straight through its closed door, until the box suspended itself before her eyes, an offering. She saw it as surely as she had seen her mother in the kitchen, cracking eggs against the side of the mixing bowl, when she used to lie alone in the tent and burn her eyes through the side of their house. Now the small, weighty gray box held firm in Roz's vision, all that remained of her mother's body, unspeakably valuable, but only to Mike and her, no one else.

There were the clothes, dumb clothes—the ones she

brought from Jefferson and the ones Mike had got ahold of for her when she moved down. What did they matter? In the sitting room, she had some chairs and tables and lamps that Mike had hauled down in the back of his pickup after they cleaned out the house in Jefferson, but they were old to begin with—they'd been given away by people who were through with them, or bought at tag sales for two or five dollars. And if Roz sold them, what would she and Mike sit on?

Joan shifted her body against the far wall of Roz's room, and her toenails clicked against the wooden floorboards. She was dreaming, Roz knew, chasing deer, streaking through the woods like light. Joan—Roz had Joan. But Roz would die before she'd sell her. Joan had come to them free but was worth more than anything. Nothing would be worth losing her, too. That was always what it came down to, though, it seemed to Roz: what you were willing to give up just to get something else. There was always a cost, like the sixty-dollar price tag on her trip to Montclair.

She stopped her inventory of things to sell, because there wasn't anything, really, just more answers that she didn't have. What Roz didn't know always towered over what she did know. And she was afraid to pile anything more onto that tower.

She concentrated instead on the comforting litany of 555-9422, area code 201—Nate Thompson's number forever, even if he had disconnected. It was like a song to Roz, that number, a prayer almost. Saying it to herself, not forgetting any part, satisfied something in Roz the way that calling Nate and hearing his voice at the end of the line had satisfied her. Or stilled her—allowed her to go to school that day, or to sleep that night. She sounded off the digits in a rhythm not unlike the songs her mother made up and sang to her, and she often lulled herself to sleep with them. She used simple things to keep the towering weight of what she didn't know from crashing down on top of her.

She couldn't know her father, any more than Ellie had known him. When Roz asked her, Ellie told her that she never saw the man, Roz's father, before or after he hurt her. "He grabbed me from behind, and he never spoke a word," Ellie told her. "The whole time. He put a pillowcase over my head while he hurt me," she said. "When I begged him not to, all my words just went into the bag. He never listened. It makes you crazy, not being listened to." Roz was almost asleep, or maybe already asleep when she remembered these things, for which she had no song.

The next morning, though, she figured out what to do about the money. It came to her while she was doing the dishes, soapy warm water almost to her elbows. Roz knew where money came from, and it wasn't from pockets or drawers. It came from work. Didn't she sit on the end of the couch and watch Mike fix busted radios and fans? Hadn't she watched her mother work her whole life?

Her mother made money doing whatever needed to be done. That was how she'd started off taking care of other people's children, before she heard her calling and opened her own school. But she picked and sold blueberries and raspberries, too. She baked and sold bread to stores in town, stores that canceled their orders once Ellie attached labels saying proceeds would benefit her school, which she called the Gathering in Love & Forgiveness.

She did some sewing for people and she cleaned houses sometimes, too. She said there was always work for people who wanted it and that honest work was blessed.

Roz scrubbed hard on the prongs of the fork. She and Mike had had eggs that morning. The words she needed to begin her journey came to her: "I'm willing to work." She was thankful for them, simple and clear words that she could repeat, words that would get things started.

On Saturday morning, she walked downtown and stood at the intersection of State and Pleasant streets. She studied the row of shops and restaurants—Pizza Connection, Beauty Supplies, Phases. It was not a long street; she could see to the STOP sign and, beyond it, the squat City Hall building across from the small park. She breathed in a promise to herself to enter every door she passed, and to tell anyone who would listen, "I am willing to work." She felt her mother with her more than ever; she felt the wooden yoke on her own shoulders, ready to carry whatever weight was put in the buckets.

But her mouth was dry. The first two places, it was all she could do to get the words out, and then she couldn't listen to what they answered, although she felt their no clearly enough. It was harder when there were other kids around, kids her own age or, worse, a little older. She thought she saw Scott "*Who* got blasted?" Ventrow at a booth in the Pizza Connection. She froze and had to will herself not to bolt back out the door. She heard a voice asking, "Can I help you? Yes?" and Roz lifted her eyes and trained them on the woman behind the counter, and made herself say, "I'm willing to work." The woman answered her with such a pretty smile that Roz wanted to lean across the counter and wrap her arms around her.

"That's real nice to hear," the woman said. "Real nice.

But I don't think there's anything open right now." At the door, Roz looked back at her and she was still smiling at Roz. "Sorry," the woman called out to her, and her voice made a song out of just that one word. Roz stepped out into the sun. It didn't matter that people were saying no. She was still moving forward.

Three-quarters of the way down the street, she turned into Prays, a fussy old department store that reminded her of clothes shops up in Lancaster, near Jefferson. The front section overflowed with pants and sweaters and skirts; there were bras and panties and nightgowns in the back. The counters around the cash register in the center of the floor were stocked with Lady Buxton wallets in dusty boxes, and fleece-lined gloves, their colored linings turned back at the wrist, small gold price tags resting daintily on the leather. From a few feet back, Roz watched a mostly bald man as he stood behind the cash register, writing fast on a clipboard.

"I'm willing to work," Roz said. She was calling to him, and she remembered to speak up.

He glanced up from his clipboard for a second and then back down. "Hold on," he told her. He continued adding up his list and then set it on the counter and addressed Roz. "So, then. What?"

"I'm willing to work," she said again.

He shrugged and his eyes closed a little and the ends of his mouth turned down.

Roz waited and hoped.

"There're some boxes that need breaking down and tying up. You interested in that? I'll give you five bucks if you do the whole pile," he said to her. "Well?"

Was she listening? Was he telling her yes? "Yes!" she fired back at him.

"Follow me," he said, and he took off like a shot. They passed a woman on their way to the stairs, and he told her, without stopping, "Lyn—watch the register, I'll be right back." They descended into Prays' lower level—a mass of curtains and pillows and what a sign, in curlicue writing, called *domestic goods*. Miniature beds with miniature windows, pairs of them covered with matching lacy spreads and curtains, jutted out from the walls of the room, dripping pastel colors and ruffles as Roz hurried under them to keep up. The mostly bald man walked very fast, through the pillow section, and back into a large, cold storeroom filled nearly to the ceiling with empty cardboard boxes, a mountain of them.

"See these?" he said to her. "See all these?" Roz nodded. Of course she did. "Okay, here's the deal," he told her. He picked up a little knife from the shelf by the door and grabbed a box from the pile. "You slit along the side here—you watching?—and then flatten it out like this, and stack it over here, you got that?" He never looked at Roz the whole time he was talking to her, but she kept nodding anyway. "Okay, once you get a pile of these, say ten, then you take this twine and wrap 'em, tight, okay?"

"Okay," Roz told him. Whatever he said. She watched him wrap the bundle and tie a quick knot, break off the twine, pulling the knife up toward himself. "Okay, then," he told her. "The whole room, five bucks, right?"

"Right."

He left her alone to work then, for which she was grateful. Everything had happened so fast. She stepped inside among the boxes and was hidden by them, and she liked that. She stood still for just a few minutes and then began her slicing and flattening and stacking. She worked carefully, flattening the unwieldy boxes, piling them together, then lopping off the right length of twine to wrap them with. She loved how ordered the room became as she made the mountain of cardboard descend. It reminded her of stacking wood, watching the heap of logs slowly diminish as she and her mother created neat rows along the side of the house.

She lost track of time. She had just finished when the balding man poked his head in to see how she was doing, and she could see that he was pleased, although he didn't say so right away.

"What'd you say your name was again?" he asked her.

She told him Roz, and he said, "Not bad at all, Roz." He reached into his pocket and pulled out a neatly folded stack, and peeled off a five-dollar bill for her. "That was the deal, right?" he said to her, and she said, "Right."

"Can I do it again?" she asked him. "Next week?" She was speaking fast. She took her cues from him, and he was fast and nervous.

"It takes me longer than that to get this far behind," he told her. "But check in and I'll see if we have anything."

That night, she sat on the end of the couch and ate Doritos out of the bag and watched a made-for-TV movie and wrestling and MTV while Mike worked on a vacuum cleaner next to her. The movie was about a boy who got kidnapped, and Roz would have happily stuck with that—the crime, the ransom note, straight through to the happy ending—but every few minutes Mike told her to cruise the tube. Every commercial, Roz thought she would tell Mike about Prays and the five dollars and how good it had felt, but every commercial came and went and she didn't. It was as if she had something to confess but didn't have the nerve. She ended up keeping it all to herself, only because she had to.

Roz counted down the whole next week just to get to Saturday. She was dying to work there again, to have the man pull out his folded bills and pay her and say, "Not bad at all, Roz." Saturday she woke up at six and hated the final three hours she had to wait before she could go downtown and work. She put on a clean pair of blue jeans and her favorite sweatshirt.

She got to the store before it even opened and waited outside, across the street, trying to look like she had something to do. After a woman unlocked the two glass doors from the inside, she made herself wait a few extra minutes before crossing the street and walking in. The bald man wasn't there and Roz didn't know what to do. The woman who had opened the door called to her, "Can I help you?" Roz felt she'd been caught at something, as if how much she wanted to work and earn her way showed all over her and made her pathetic somehow. She didn't know what to say. She didn't even know the man's name. "I'm willing to work," she blurted out.

The woman said, "We wouldn't have anything," and immediately turned away from Roz. The words hit her hard. Everything was over so quickly, after so much hope. She made her feet turn and carry her toward the door. The bald man was just walking in. He raised his eyebrows and gave her a smile, but breezed right by her. He did a double take, though. "It's you, yeah. What's your name?"

"Roz."

"Right. Roz. I knew that. You lookin' for more work?"

Roz nodded, bright. She hoped the woman behind the counter was watching. She hated that woman.

"Nah," he said, "nothin' this week. But keep trying."
Roz pushed against the door with all her weight to get
out. But just as she was leaving, the man called after her,
"You're so hot to work, get a paper route. I had a paper
route for years when I was your age. Years."

She stood out on the sidewalk and let his words sink
in. A paper route.

So many things came as news to Roz—the simplest,
most obvious things! Why didn't she know things that
other people did? And he had said it as if it were nothing,
but it was everything. She loved the bald man. She re-
traced her steps on Pleasant Street, and made her way
over to the Daily News Building on Liberty Street. When
she passed by the Pizza Connection she looked in at the
woman who had smiled and sung "Sorry" to her, and
Roz loved her, too.

Ten days later, Roz started her paper route. She took
it as nothing less than a miracle: getting what she needed,
and getting it so soon. It was as if things were fair, as if
there were some sort of bigger plan that took care of it
all, just as her mother had always promised her.

This time, with this piece of news, telling Mike was
no problem. And he got a kick out of it. He said, "A
paper route, no kiddin'?" about five times, and came
home from the grocery store that night with two lobsters
for dinner, to celebrate. Before he plunged them into the
boiling water he said, "Sie-onara." Roz hated that part
—the plunge—but it was her favorite food. Mike put a
whole roll of paper towels on the table and they ripped
off wads of it to mop up the butter that ran down their
chins and greased their hands. Mike told her that pretty
soon she'd be the one buying lobster, with all the money
she'd be raking in.

The following Friday and Saturday, Roz accompanied the boy who was giving up the route she'd be taking over. It ran down Greenleaf and around Pond and back up to State, a triangle of twenty-seven customers. She met Jimmy Matthews, a short fifth grader, at his house on Dalton Street, where the papers were dropped off every afternoon and Saturday morning.

He was loading them into his canvas carrier when Roz tapped him on the shoulder, and he pulled up and gave her a bothered look. Roz didn't know if he was mad that he had to take a girl with him while he delivered, or if he was just one of those boys who always acted bothered by everything. "Follow me," he said, and he didn't speak again, except for the few times he begrudgingly told her something about the customers. Even then he didn't turn to look at her, but just spoke out into the open air: "Put it on the side porch." "Their dog is wicked mean." "They always need change when you collect."

Roz had a vague understanding that he had no right to act as if he were doing her a favor—she was a grade ahead of him, and much bigger—but she didn't care. She was studying each house, memorizing the number of porch stairs, looking to see how Jimmy collected money and marked *Paid* in his little green account book. All Roz wanted was to learn the route, and take it over as her own.

Saturday morning, after they had finished collecting, she and Jimmy walked in silence to the Daily News Building and gave their payment for the week to the woman behind the desk, Mrs. Walker. All the extra, the tip money, went to Jimmy. He shoved the dollars and change into his pocket, and then snapped the canvas bag and green account book up to Roz's face and said, "Here," and that was it: the changing of the guard, transfer of power. Roz had her own route.

The next Monday, the papers were dropped off at her house, and she delivered solo for the first time. She loaded the papers into the canvas bag and lifted it onto her shoulder. It was heavy when she started out, but she didn't mind, she even liked it. She thought about her mother with the yoke, hauling water.

Before she fell asleep at night, after she listened for the prayer that still had not come, she completed the route all over again: the twenty-seven stops, the white house, the back doors, the porch steps that wobbled. A few nights she didn't even need Nate Thompson's number to lull her to sleep. Some nights she dreamed the route as well, and she remembered those dreams, and they definitely weren't nightmares.

On Friday and Saturday, she made her first collection—$1.80 a week from each customer. The first woman, Mrs. Trembly, gave Roz two dollars and said to keep the change. The next customer, Mrs. Burton, gave her $2.50. So did Mr. Leary. She marked everyone who paid in the green account book, putting a neat check next to their names, and tried to remember to say thank you and give them the paper even though it was a lot to do. She was shaking inside at all the money she was handling.

After she'd taken the money to Mrs. Walker at the News Building, she went home to count what was left over, what Ellie would have called "rightfully hers." Up in her room, leaning against the bed, she counted out the dollars and change over and over. She had cleared $13.75. She stacked the coins in neat, leaning towers of silver against the walls of her cigar-box bank, and smoothed and flattened the dollar bills. She felt herself racing toward lift-off, she saw the *Challenger* about to go up, the arrow soon to fly.

She got through each day of school just waiting to get to the stack of papers and deliver them. By the second week she knew the route inside out. She knew the number of porch steps, the exact pitch of the dog's bark, the face of each of her customers. What she had not counted on, but what happened, was that people got to know her, too. Roz tended to think about things from one side— what she was seeing, and not that she was being seen. So it surprised her when people going by on State Street waved to her from their cars, and greeted her by name on Friday when she came to collect. She was surprised, but she liked it. Roz was a little embarrassed about how much she liked it, how it kind of thrilled her when Mrs. Burton told her "Come on inside, sweetie," while she looked for her purse so that she could pay Roz, and how much she liked standing inside other people's living rooms, rooms with books, and flower-patterned covers on the chairs, and framed pictures of the kids the whole length of the stairway. It was as if she became part of something, just by having a paper route. It was as if she had a normal life.

After a while, she did not think about why she had the route, or what exactly the money she was accumulating was for. It was just the route itself that satisfied her: the work of hauling and putting down and taking collection money and talking to Mrs. Walker at the *Daily News*. On her fifth Saturday collection, though, Roz went over the sixty-dollar mark. She knew, as she was making change for Mrs. Driscoll, that these were the dollars that would do it. It struck her again how much could go on inside a person and not show. She thanked Mrs. Driscoll and handed her the paper, as if nothing at all had happened, even though everything had changed.

She got the urge to kneel again, the way that she had after she got her period. Everything hit her at once—what she had to do, what she had to be willing to give up, the dread again, too—and it was enough to buckle her knees. But she had seven papers left to deliver, and she was making her way around the newly renovated condominiums on Pond Street, out in the open, in the middle of the world, and she just kept going.

When she finished the route, she took her money to the *Daily News* office and turned it in to Mrs. Walker. "This is my last week," Roz told her, pushing her bag of money over the desk counter. "I have to give it up."

"What?" Mrs. Walked cocked her head as she zoomed in on Roz. "So soon? Roz, you just started, and you've done such a lovely job."

Roz wanted Mrs. Walker to stop talking, to not say one thing.

"I have to," she said.

"But why, Roz?"

"I have to go away," Roz told her. She hadn't counted on having to say why.

"Go away?" Mrs. Walker said, so concerned that Roz could tell it showed that she was about to cry. "Are you moving, Roz?"

"No," Roz said, "I just have to go away for a few days." She was telling her so much more than she meant to, than felt safe.

"Well, for how long, Roz?"

"Two days," Roz answered her.

"Oh, Roz," Mrs. Walker said, with a relieved laugh, and she brought her hand up and laid it across her chest.

"You don't have to give up your route just because of a few days. Everyone goes away now and then."

Roz stared at her and could hardly believe what she was hearing. She did not have to give it up? Like Abraham not having to sacrifice Isaac, Roz was being spared? The relief was so enormous, so grand, flooding her the same way it did every time her mother read her the story, and Isaac didn't have to die after all.

"Oh, darling," Mrs. Walker continued. "Two days is *nothing*." She leaned in closer to Roz, and put her hand over Roz's. "Just have one of your friends cover for you."

Roz froze. It was the worst feeling of all—the one that took her along, included her for the ride up until the very end, and then dropped her, cold. As if everyone in the whole world had a friend, had a bunch of them to choose from, as if it was just like breathing to have friends.

Mrs. Walker was watching Roz. "Or we could ask one of the other carriers to take your route for those two days. We could do that. When is it you'll be away?"

It didn't really matter. "Monday and Tuesday," she answered, her voice flat.

"Well, I'm sure I can find someone," Mrs. Walker said. "Okay?"

Roz nodded and couldn't even say thank you.

Mrs. Walker counted out the money from her collection purse and handed the rest back to Roz. "We can't afford to lose one of our best carriers, now can we?" Mrs. Walker said, so bright it hurt Roz's eyes. Things could seem normal, but it didn't mean they were.

Six

When Roz got home, she threw her money into the cigar box and then went to get her camping gear from the basement. She was anxious to keep going, afraid that if she stopped now she might stop altogether. She went quickly and quietly into the dank, semi-darkness of their cellar—sneaking, almost, though Mike wasn't even home—to the shelf where he had stored Ellie's and her camping equipment. She reached up and pulled down the nylon pouch that held her sleeping bag and clutched it against her chest like a baby. Her mother's backpack, bright orange on its metal frame, lay deflated on the shelf, its cords hanging limp over the side. The pack looked huge to Roz, but she planned to use it, imagined that when she finally swung it onto her back, it would fit, somehow.

She carried the backpack and sleeping bag and tent up from the basement and put them in her room. She thought she might unroll the tent and check and make sure all the pieces were there, but suddenly she couldn't. She had done enough, maybe even more than enough, for one day, and she was tired. She stood and just stared at the brightly colored nylon, wrapped tight, and felt her shoulders drop a foot. How would she ever pull it off?

Just have one of your friends cover for you, she heard, a whisper in her head, and she couldn't stand it. She gathered everything and opened her closet door and jammed it all in and then held the door closed, as if it might try and push its way out.

She flopped across her bed and buried her face in the bedspread. After a while she turned her head and lay quietly, waiting for the crunch of Mike's tires on their driveway gravel. He'd come home and call out "You here, Roz?" and she'd go down and they'd decide what to do about dinner.

Roz had gone over to Mike's way of being about food. All that mattered to Mike was having enough and having it taste good. With Ellie, what mattered was that it *be* good—holy, almost. Roz remembered how her mother reached into the oven with the hot pad and pulled out the loaves of bread, how she sliced off the end piece and swiped it with butter that melted right into its pores. As Roz took the first bite, Ellie would stand with her hands clasped together as if she were praying, until Roz smiled and let out a low hum of pleasure. Food with Mike was faster, and there was more of it, and not a lot of watching each other.

Mike came home and they made spaghetti with tomato sauce, and toasted big hunks of Italian bread with cheese sprinkled on them, and ate ice cream sandwiches for dessert. Then they cruised the tube while Mike worked on somebody's Dustbuster. Roz could stay up as late as she wanted on the weekends. She wanted to stay up the whole night, to be awake for every minute of her last weekend before she had to go, but by the eleven o'clock news her eyelids were too heavy to hold open. She wished hours didn't zoom by as she slept. She knew those hours were carrying her right up to the doorstep of her taking off.

Sunday afternoon, she loaded the backpack with the tent and sleeping bag, threw in her rain jacket and another sweatshirt and her flashlight and some wadded-up toilet paper, and zippered her money into the front pocket. She yanked the cords tight and then hoisted the pack onto her back. It was big, but she could manage. She didn't even feel its weight. While Mike was making a delivery, she carried the pack outside and stashed it behind the lilac bushes, and then retreated from it, hurried back to her room.

That night, she dreamed endlessly that she had overslept, missed her bus, forgotten her backpack, lost her money. When she awakened, the feeling of dread was pulsing all through her. She hoped it was a nightmare she could leave behind, but she knew she was awake, that screaming would not help. Her body weighed a thousand pounds lying in her bed, in the dark. She wondered how she would ever pick it up and move it all the way to Montclair, New Jersey.

With all her heart, she wished that she could go wake up Mike and tell him what she was going to do, have some cocoa, fish. She wished she could wake up in the tent and turn in her sleeping bag and see her mother there. She wouldn't even need to touch her, just to see her sleeping body next to hers. Her mother would never have left the tent if she knew that it scared Roz. She would never have done that. But Roz didn't tell her that she was scared. She didn't ask her not to leave the tent. Her mother would never have taken off that morning, searching for Nate, if she'd known that Roz would wake up and be scared, even more scared when she went into the kitchen and no one was there.

Daybreak slowly seeped its way into Roz's bedroom, and the light made things real: her chest of drawers, the curtains, her slightly open closet door. She heard Mike climb out of bed and walk to the bathroom. She threw back her blanket.

Roz met Mike in the hall, as he was coming out, his old blue jeans hanging loose and low around his big middle. He was scratching his head and said, "Mornin'," when he passed by.

"Hi, Mike."

"How about I make a run for doughnuts?"

While he was out, Roz sat on her bed and wrote him a note. She hadn't planned to, but she couldn't leave without a word.

> *Mike,*
> *I have to go do something. Be back late tomorrow.*
> *Love, Roz.*

Her words looked puny on the page. She wished she could draw something, something that would finish it, make it clear, but no picture came to her. She thought she had said as much as she could, but then suddenly added, down at the bottom, *Don't be scared.* She took it into Mike's bedroom, across the hall, and laid it on the heap of blankets at the bottom of his unmade bed.

Mike came back and they ate their breakfast rolls and

Mike listened to the morning news. Roz made her lunch. Just before she folded down the bag to close it, she dropped in some of the doughnut holes Mike had brought back with him. It was as much to take Mike along with her as to eat them. Then she sponged off the counter, and said, even though it was earlier than usual, "Well, I better go."

Mike told her, the way he did every day, "Another day at the salt mines." He was pouring himself a second cup of coffee.

Joan lay against the back door. Roz walked over to her and patted her bony head. "You can't come," she whispered. She often said that to Joan when she left for school, but today it struck Roz as mean, leaning down to whisper, "You can't come," to her friend. "You stay," she amended. "I'll be back."

As soon as she stood alone on the back porch, separated by just a door and a wall from Mike and Joan, the day began in a whole new way for Roz. The morning was bright and already warm. Weather was something that Roz didn't usually notice unless it was especially bad. Now it struck her that weather mattered a lot. She took the bright morning as a good sign, and felt her strength coming back into her; she felt her mother. Near the side of the house she pulled the backpack out from the bushes. Its metal frame was cold, the knots hard as she loosed them to open the top flap and drop in her paper-bagged lunch.

Roz hoisted the backpack and snapped the belt around her hips. So, she thought, this is what my mother always carried. This and more. Roz walked around the far side of the house and took a right on State Street, so there'd be no chance of Mike catching sight of her through the shop window. At the intersection of High and State, she took a left and started her trek to the bus stop, a little more than two miles away. It was early enough that not too many other kids were on the street yet. She was glad for that. She looked down so that she would not see any of the faces in the passing cars, as if not looking at people protected her from being seen, and blocked out everything except her footsteps, one after the other. Deep down, Roz had the feeling that she should walk all the way to New Jersey, that she should make the trip on her own two feet. She knew it was crazy. No one walked to New Jersey. But there was something so solid about it, the way her sneakers hit the pavement, step after step, the same way she and her mother had hiked together, that appealed to her, and made her think it was the way to go. Her mother had taught her, the only way to know a place is to walk it.

The weight of the backpack settled in on Roz soon enough, though. The frame hung too low on her and rubbed a bit against her thigh with each step. She got hot. But she felt she couldn't afford to stop and peel off her denim jacket and stuff it in her pack. She heard her mother's high, thin voice, singing a song from her Girl Scout days, "I'm hap-py when I'm hik-ing." She always sang it just when Roz *wasn't* happy, when she wanted to stop, take another drink, when she thought they would never get to the top. It always made them laugh, that song, and it always kept Roz going.

The bus stop finally came into sight up ahead of her, just before the entrance to I-95, and Roz was nothing but relieved. Her spirit was willing to walk to New Jersey, but her pack was heavy and her feet were already tired. She wished, then, as she walked the final hundred yards, that she could fly to New Jersey, lift off the ground, pack and all, and fly there, straight, as the crow flies. How much she would rather swoop down on Nate Thompson, from out of the sky, like a low-flying heron, than board a big, clunky, smelly bus. She reached back and hoisted the frame of her pack, so that for just an instant the weight was lifted off her shoulders.

A small group of people was waiting in front of the trailer that served as the Newburyport bus station. Roz walked behind them and climbed the steps to the trailer door and pushed it open. She could barely make it over the threshold with her pack on; she had to turn sideways to squeeze through the narrow frame. The woman behind the counter stared wordlessly at Roz as she unclipped the hip belt and unloaded her pack, and Roz wished that she could be invisible, not hot and struggling with an over-sized pack, being watched. Where was her clean and easy getaway? Her mother had done it—just slipped out of sight—but she was not her mother. Roz unzipped the front flap and pulled out sixty dollars in neatly folded bills and held them in her hand. Her face was beet red. "I need to go to Montclair, New Jersey, from New-buryport," she told the woman behind the counter. Her old lines came back to her.

"By yourself?" the woman said.

Fear made Roz answer fast. "I'm meeting my mother there," she said without thinking. She was glad her face had been red to start with.

The woman didn't seem to care one way or the other. "We'll get you to New York," she told Roz. "Get the rest of your ticket there."

Roz's heart sank. She wanted to hand over all the money, not do it bit by bit.

"One-way or round-trip?"

The woman was going too fast. Roz didn't have all the answers. She didn't know what the woman was asking her. Finally the woman said, "You stayin' where you're goin', or you wanna come back?"

"Oh," Roz breathed out in relief, "I want to come back home." She counted out $51.95 for the woman and got her ticket. As she stepped aside, she noticed for the first time the boxes of candy bars beneath the glass countertop: Snickers, Baby Ruths, Almond Joys. She wanted a Baby Ruth badly, as badly as she had ever wanted anything, it seemed, but she had missed her chance. She couldn't make herself speak up and ask for it.

She waited outside with the others for the bus, filled with mourning for the sweet, nutty chocolate she wasn't eating, the candy bar she always chose when she and her mother went to the movies in Lancaster. She promised to treat herself to one later, in Boston, or New York, or Montclair. She knew she wouldn't, but the stab of pain passed anyway.

The bus driver stowed her backpack underneath the bus, and Roz felt light and a little empty without it. She chose a seat toward the front of the bus, next to a short, pudgy woman with two shopping bags at her feet who started talking to Roz even before Roz had settled in.

"Might as well unbutton right now," she said, nodding at Roz's jacket. "Nothing's worse than being hot in a bus."

Roz smiled and dutifully pulled apart the silver snaps.

"Except being cold in a bus," the woman continued. "And I've been in plenty of cold buses, I'm here to tell you."

The woman, Mrs. Eugenie Dimato, from Salisbury, on her way to Boston to see a podiatrist, was there to tell Roz a lot of things. She never stopped talking the whole time. In traffic on the Tobin Bridge, she told Roz about her oldest daughter Eleanor's wedding, the five-tiered cake that she, Eugenie, had baked herself after taking a special course in cake baking that was offered in Manchester. She was telling Roz about her second oldest daughter's wedding, the bridesmaids' dresses, when they pulled into the station in Boston, and Roz sat and waited for her to finish describing the three-quarter-length sleeves while the other passengers made their way down the center aisle and out of the bus.

"So," she finally finished up, "now you know," as if Roz had asked and Eugenie had only done her duty in answering her. Roz was free to go.

Roz thanked her and told her goodbye, and then claimed her backpack. When she entered the terminal, she had to remind herself that she was already in Boston, that far along, because she felt she had done so little to get herself there. It seemed that the trip had carried on almost without her, while she was off in someone else's life, with a wedding cake and bridesmaids' dresses. It hit her, then, how ready she was for the trip to be hard, for things to go wrong, and be dangerous. What she hadn't counted on was smooth sailing.

Roz waited for the New York bus in an orange plastic seat next to Gate 7. She rested her backpack against her feet and legs and watched the other people. Some of them stared at little TV sets that were bolted to the arms of their chairs. Roz hated those TVs. What were they doing there? How would anyone know when their buses came? What if they missed them? The chairs with the attached sets pulled her, all the same. She could feel the pile of change in her pockets. She could put some in the slot and find a movie or a game show. She could cruise the tube.

Roz remembered the bag of doughnut holes she had added to her lunch bag, and reached for them now. She drew out a cinnamon one, already slightly stale and dry. The cinnamon dust caught in her throat and made her cough, but she just kept eating. When she was finished with one she took another and then another and another, eating as fast as she could, shoving them in her mouth until she had eaten them all. When her thirst hit, it was so big she wanted to cry. She had eaten all the doughnuts, and she had nothing to drink, and she had made herself a little sick.

She went to the bathroom and cupped water from the faucet into her hands and drank that, even though it tasted terrible. The bathroom smelled like poison to her, and every noise, every cough and flush and unlatching of the stall door, echoed loud and ugly off the walls. The room scared her and she hurried back out, her hands still dripping wet. She folded them together in her lap and tried to stop the sinking she felt inside, as if some plug had been pulled and all her strength was draining out. Soon it would be spilled, lost, over the side of the mountain, and then where would she be?

When she heard the call for her bus, Roz jerked her pack up and was among the first in line to hand over her ticket and board. She took a seat up front for herself, next to the window, and hoped she'd be left alone. She promised herself not to be detoured by words again, or food, or anything. It hit her that *this* was the time to fast—not before. Fasting around Mike was crazy. "Not eat?" Roz could see his open, flat face. But she was with her mother now, on her way to find out about her mother. Mike wouldn't have to see her not eating and she'd save money, too. It was a good idea, fasting, and it stopped the sinking feeling inside her a bit. She was sorry that she had believed, even for a minute, in the possibility of smooth sailing.

A woman in a green skirt and jacket sat down next to Roz. She smiled briefly and then opened her *Boston Globe,* leaning her head into the Living Section. Roz studied the woman's legs, the golden brownish glint of her nylons and the puffy thickness of the sneakers, like little couches wrapped around her feet. Those sneakers were the last thing she saw: Roz was asleep before the bus was back on the highway, her head lolling over toward the window. But even in her sleep, dreaming a string of disconnected stories, Roz never let herself go entirely. And when she woke up, and stared for hours out the window, she was silently vigilant about what she was doing and where she was going, until the bus made its final turn into Port Authority.

The terminal was big and crowded and smelled like hot dogs and grease. Roz followed the signs toward Information. On the escalator she had, for just a second, the suspended feeling she had known with her mother, crossing the bridge, and she soared with it. She watched the people around her, going down as she was riding up, and then in the grand concourse, everyone on their way somewhere, as if they knew where they were headed. No one tried to kidnap her. No one had knives or guns. She found out everything she needed to know at the information window in the main booking hall, as if people had been set on earth, at that very place, to guide her along the way. She felt the yoke on her shoulder, her buckets filled with water that was weighty but balanced, and that she could carry. She bought her ticket to Montclair and took the escalator up to Gate 413.

She saw him as soon as she turned the corner. He sat slumped against a concrete pillar, as if someone had poured him there. She froze.

"Change," he said to her. His voice was gravelly and low. He lifted his hand. "Change?"

Why was he asking her? What could she do? The man had hair like matted fur, his body was dressed in too many clothes—a huge checkered coat, a limp wool cap that nearly covered his eyes. Change? He jabbed his hand toward her again. "Spare some change, kid?" he said.

So it was money he wanted. That change. But how would she get it to him? She would have to walk closer, bend down to him, reach out her hand. Even standing where she was, Roz could smell him. She pulled back slightly and startled at the stream of people flooding by on their way to the upper level, none of them stopping, or even looking at the man slumped against the pillar, his hand held out to Roz. With just a step, just the slightest turn, she was back in the stream, and past him.

He followed her, though. His face stayed just ahead of her own, his outstretched palm. She burrowed her right hand into her jacket pocket and felt the coins she could easily have reached in and given him, but hadn't. Why not? Only because she was scared, because she'd been taken by surprise. A story jabbed at her, what was it? Jesus was a beggar, and people passed him by because they did not see him for who he really was. Oh, God, had she just walked by Jesus?

Roz stopped, and a man plowed into her from behind. "Excuse me!" he said, grabbing her by the shoulders and steadying her. But he was off again, on his way to the platforms, and Roz turned into the tide of people rushing forward, and went back to the man slumped against the pillar.

She came up to the side of him, digging in both pockets and clutching what she found inside her fists. She leaned down and said, "I do have some change." He turned and stared at her. His eyes were a filmy blue, as if they were out of focus. Roz could see they held no memory—that he did not remember having just spoken to her, or that she had walked away. The man probably wasn't Jesus—surely Jesus would recognize *her*, she thought—but it didn't matter anymore.

She showed him the piles of coins she held. He slowly raised a long, graceful hand, dirty, with the longest fingernails Roz had ever seen on a man. They were thick and yellow. Roz brought both her hands together and dropped her wrists so that the coins cascaded from her hands into his, without Roz ever touching him at all. She straightened up and looked down on what she had given him and wished she had more to offer.

He slid his hand with all the coins into the pocket of his huge coat, and brought it out empty, and held it back up to Roz. He was not asking for more, she realized. He wanted her to shake it. She drew in her breath and extended her hand and gave him one short, strong clasp. "Goodbye," she said.

Her backpack bounced up and down as she hurried up the final escalator, doing double time to the slow-moving mechanical steps. Suddenly she was afraid that she would miss the bus, that it would roll out of its long, narrow parking place without her, leaving her to stand in clouds of gassy exhaust. But she saw it as soon as she reached the top and ran to Gate 413—the big, hulking bus that would deliver her to Nate.

Seven

Roz and her mother always found the perfect campsite when they slept out. Ellie Jacoby said that she was led to it—that the place chose her, and not the other way around. She said all she ever did was trust that it would be there.

Roz tried to trust, too, but her first views of Montclair, through the bus window, offered her nothing at all. Was she supposed to trust in nothing? Every place she saw was already taken: lived in, built up with big houses with porches and garages, and strings of little stores, and sidewalks. There wasn't a hint of space, secret and protected, that called to Roz or invited her to set up camp.

Then, on her left, the park came into view, its grassy slope so green and perfect that it seemed a carpet rising up and extending back into a stand of trees and flowering bushes. The emerald hill was dreamlike, and almost without thinking Roz raised her arm and pulled down the wire cord that ran above the seats of the bus. A ping sounded and at the next corner the bus pulled over and breathed open its doors in a whoosh. The man who had been sitting next to Roz helped her lift down her backpack from the overhead rack, and out of nowhere—they hadn't even spoken on the trip from New York—he told her, "Good luck."

What he said frightened Roz. She was suddenly afraid that something showed on her—her life, or what was missing from it, or that she was alone. She didn't want —couldn't afford, really—for anything to show, and she tried, as she stepped out of the bus, to draw herself in somehow so that she didn't give anything away. The effort of doing that—almost like trying to erase herself—made her feel as if she were walking backward, even as she plodded ahead toward the park. The road was filled with traffic in both directions—people on their way home, she knew. She lowered her head and pretended that she had a destination, too.

"Montclair," she chanted to herself, "Montclair," in and out with every breath. It confused her to change places quickly, all in a day. Where was she? She breathed "Montclair" as she veered off on the blacktopped path that led up to the wooded plateau. "Boston," she had hummed to herself in that terminal, and then "New York," waiting to buy her ticket at Port Authority, and now "Montclair, Montclair."

She was drawn toward a row of rhododendron bushes, all in flower, massive pink blooms bursting from their tapered leaves. She pushed between two of the bushes to a small clearing, a triangle of land just large enough to pitch her tent. Two Miller beer bottles lay on their sides on the pine-needled ground. She remembered her mother gathering whatever trash she found in the places where they camped, stowing it in her backpack, and then carrying it out in the morning. Maybe the bottles were a sign. Roz squatted down and set them upright and considered the little plot of ground. It seemed the right place, but how could she be certain? Her mother was the only person who could be absolutely sure.

She pulled open the drawstring pouch and shook out the wrapped cylinder of bright orange nylon. Lightweight stakes scattered around her like oversized bullets. She had always put it up with her mother, staking the front while her mother staked the back, pulling the roof line taut.

Now she did it on her own. She staked one end, and then the other, but nothing snapped to attention; no part of the tent rose up and declared itself. The stakes wouldn't go down as deep as she wanted them to. She got hot pounding on them, tossed her jacket over by the beer bottles, and kept at it, but finally, without her mother there to help, had to settle for less. She crawled inside and dragged her pack in after her and stayed there, kneeling on all fours, with her head dropped down, like a dog who'd done something bad.

She had not been in the tent since Jefferson, since the last time she'd slept out with her mother in the field behind their house. Roz remembered all over again how her mother had been gone when Roz awakened. She remembered her mother being gone more clearly than anything else.

Roz had told herself that Ellie was in the house, starting breakfast. Or maybe walking—she had taken to long walks again—but she would be back. Back, Roz told herself, before Roz had even taken out the eggs and mixing bowl, and she would wrap her arms around Roz and say, "Did you dream?"

That morning, the morning her mother died, when Roz had pushed open the flap of the tent and looked across the field to their house, she hadn't been able to make her eyes burn through the clapboards and beams into the kitchen. She had lost that power of hers. She pulled on her sneakers and raced across the slippery grass, wet with dew, straight to the kitchen door.

The cold of the kitchen jolted her—it felt colder inside than out without the warmth of the cookstove to greet her. She stood still on the threshold and listened to the absolute quiet of the room. She knew her mother was not there, as surely as she'd known her mother was not in the tent beside her. She did not even bother to call out, "Mom?" as if she might answer, from the bathroom, or upstairs. The house was empty and cold and Roz backed out of it, stepping down onto the granite slab outside the kitchen door. She turned and surveyed as much land as she could take in. Red-winged blackbirds were out, and swallows.

Roz stood on the granite step, and the more scared she got, the stiller she stood. Don't be scared, she told herself. She willed herself to turn and open the door and go in the house and start breakfast herself, as if nothing had happened, nothing had changed. Roz would be there, cracking eggs on the side of the bowl, when her mother walked through the field and pulled open the door, and Roz would ask her first, "Did you dream?"

She stepped back into the kitchen, ready, this time, for how cold it would be. Sunlight wasn't yet streaming through the north-facing windows, but switching on a light would have scared her more, so she didn't. She drew out the carton of brown eggs from the squat refrigerator with the heavy door, and lifted down a mixing bowl from the nest of bowls on the shelf over the sink. Standing in semi-darkness at the long wooden table, she took the first egg and tapped it against the rim of the bowl. The sound was hollow and sad. She pried her thumbs into the crack she had made and slowly pulled the shell into halves, gently dropping the golden eye and its pool of gel into the bowl. Then she took the next one. This time she gave a shorter, sharper rap against the side, so that the crack was deeper, more defined, and she pulled the shell apart without making chips or fragments. She took the next egg and then the next, until she stood with the whole box of them cracked and opened into the bowl, a dozen golden wet eyes, some of them round and firm, others spreading, leaking out of shape. She wished there were a million eggs to crack, enough eggs to fill all the time in the world. But when she saw that she had emptied the box she took the whisk, the big one her mother used, the one her mother wielded with such power. Ellie could stir anything with that whisk—batter that was thick and heavy, clotted with flour—and keep it moving. With just a few drops of water or milk or oil her mother could make the batter moist, answerable to the rhythm and power of her stirring. Ellie had told Roz so many times, "I am answerable only to God." Now Roz wondered, where did a person go to answer God? And how long did it take? If her mother was gone—really gone this time—then God had called her, and she had answered. Who would not answer God?

Roz took the whisk and it felt big in her hand, too thick at its base. She started to beat the eggs. Her hand, without her mother's to close over it and motor her movements, felt awkward, undirected. Some of the egg rose up along the side of the bowl, some spilled out over the edge as Roz made her sweeps with the whisk. Roz hated it and she stopped, left the whisk sitting in the pool of eggs, pulled out the stool from under the table, and sat. She waited, in the house, ten hours.

Now she was waiting in Montclair, New Jersey, and it was night that loomed in front of Roz, eternal. The sun had not even begun to set. She backed out of the tent, into soft early-summer light. She stood and observed, with shame, what she'd set up—the tent, slightly dipping across the top, its sides concave like sunken cheeks. A huge growl twisted up through her body. She had not eaten since the doughnut holes in Boston, had not drunk since she'd cupped foul water from the bathroom faucet. Suddenly, more than anything else, she wanted Mike's sloppy joes—what he called goop. She could smell the concoction, loaded with tomatoes and hamburger and celery; she could see Mike in the kitchen ladling more than the bun could hold onto its soft white face. She wanted goop, or she wanted Mike? She was hungry for everything.

Roz grabbed her jacket, backed away from the tent, and pushed her way out through the rhododendron bushes. Standing at the top of the hill, looking down at the street, she felt herself teetering. In a second, she let loose and began sailing down the grassy slope, picking up speed as she gave herself over to it. Her arms rose out to the side automatically—to brake her speed or make her sail even faster? It didn't matter. When she reached the street, she knew she'd find a phone and call Mike, just to let him know she'd bought round-trip tickets.

The man at the White Hen Pantry told Roz the phone was located next to the milk coolers. As he spoke, she studied the Slush Puppie machine and the coffee stand behind him. To the right, on the counter, the day's leftover doughnuts and éclairs rested on one another underneath a plastic lid. Roz had a hard time turning her back on them. She could not figure what she wanted more, or first: Mike's voice, or food.

"Thanks," she told the man, and started back toward the phone—hungriest, after all, for a voice. She grabbed the receiver off its hook and held it in one hand as she groped inside her jacket pocket with the other. She burrowed in her empty pocket for a few seconds before she realized—and it snuck up behind her and grabbed her just below the ribs—that she had given away her change. Roz had given the man by the pillar all she had.

She let out a moan and lowered her head, still holding the phone in her hand. How could she need something so much and not get it? She bounced up and down on the balls of her feet and hummed—just one note, a low sound, not a song.

Roz had hummed when the woman told her about her mother. The light had changed in the kitchen, though the chill hadn't entirely lifted. Finally a voice had called out from the front door, "Hello? Hello? Anybody home?"

The voice kept calling out, "Anyone here?" as it came closer to Roz, down the narrow hallway and into the kitchen. The woman startled when she saw Roz. "Oh, oh, I'm sorry. You're here. You scared me."

Don't be scared, Roz told herself. She started humming, she looked down at the triangle of wooden seat she saw between her legs. It was the color of dried blood, and chipping. She could feel her mother a million miles away.

"Roz?" the woman began. "Do you remember me?" Roz did not remember. The woman laid the lightest hand across Roz's back. Had she dreamed her? Who was she? "Darling," she said, "I'm so sorry." So, the woman was sorry. "There's been an accident," she said. "There's been a terrible accident and your mother fell on the mountain."

Roz began to pick at one of the paint chips on the stool seat. It flicked off and down to the floor. The woman was touching her more, she had her arm across Roz's back, her hand squeezing Roz's shoulder. She introduced herself again: "I'm so sorry."

Roz shrugged.

"She was trying to save the lost boy, the hiker who was lost on the mountain. She must have slipped. She fell, Roz. I'm so sorry, she fell trying to save the boy."

Roz saw Isaac, with his bundle of firewood. Had her mother made a sacrifice? What boy? Roz hummed louder, one note, one word—*boy*.

The woman told her that Mike was on his way, that her uncle would be there soon, and that Roz should come home with her, and wait for him there.

But no part of Roz rose up to go with the woman, away from the kitchen or the house, even further away from her mother. The woman tugged gently on Roz, but Roz leveled such a furious look at her that the woman drew back her hands as if she had burned them.

Roz remembered the woman's hands. She looked down at her own, then slammed the receiver back in its cradle and took off, out of the store, right past the Slush Puppie machine and the doughnuts. Her stomach just hurt now; she didn't call it hunger. She raced back to the park as if someone were waiting there for her, as if she were late. She did not stop running until she had reached the grassy slope, and then she stood, slightly bent over, panting. A few people flowed by her along the path—joggers, a woman pushing a baby in a stroller, all of them heading straight toward the sun. It had finally begun to set.

Roz straightened and watched as it sank, big and round, behind the hill. It hit her, then, that it had been only one day: the sun was setting on the same day that she had started out with Mike and Joan in the kitchen. How could she have gone so far away—farther than she'd imagined—in so little time? It felt like forever, it felt a thousand hours long, but it hadn't been much time at all. If Mike was waiting for her in the kitchen, he hadn't waited long. She felt inside her pocket for all she had left: her round-trip tickets home.

Once the sun had disappeared completely, she walked back to the tent and crawled inside. The only thing to do was wait—she knew that now. She took out the flashlight from the front pocket, just to have it ready for when it got dark, and discovered the lunch she had made for herself that morning, a hundred years ago. She had forgotten all about it, and now she forgot about fasting, forgot that her mother said that sometimes it helped her to love, and she devoured the lunch. She was kneeling, dropped back on her heels, rocking some. She was still humming a little, even as she ate, the way Joan sometimes growled when she inhaled her Alpo, as if a pack of hungry dogs were right behind her, about to descend. Roz stuffed the cookies down first, and then gobbled the peanut-butter-and-jelly sandwich, drank the warm tropical punch drink from its box container. Eventually she stopped her humming, and was quiet, and then even full. She decided just to stay where she was, in the tent, and not move. It was early to be there—real night hadn't come on yet—but all she could think to do was hold still.

Roz would not even move from the stool after the woman told her that her mother had fallen. Where was there to go? Finally the woman said that they could wait there together, that that would be fine, but she needed to make a call. She went into the living room and turned her back to Roz and lowered her voice as she spoke on the phone, but Roz could hear her anyway. She heard her say, "Have the uncle come here." And she heard her say, "I don't know how much she took in, how much she understands." She was talking as if Roz had heard wrong, or not enough. Roz understood that her mother was answerable only to God. She knew sometimes her mother was called away from her. She knew about falling. Did the woman understand?

Right before the woman hung up, Roz heard her say, "No, she won't budge. She's her mother's daughter."

Roz could not get warm inside her sleeping bag, inside the tent. It was not a cold night—there was a mugginess to the air that promised all of summer in it—and it was warmer than many nights Roz had spent outside with her mother, but cold had seeped into her and she couldn't get around it. She put on the extra sweatshirt she'd packed, then placed her hands between her thighs and rounded her body, head drawing into her knees. It was all she could do to keep her teeth from chattering.

When night finally settled in, it turned up the volume on every single sound Roz heard, and she heard lots of them, all around her, outside the tent. People, she knew, not animals. She wasn't afraid. She told herself not to be. People were scarier than animals, though, always ready to bite with their stupid questions: was she listening, did she understand? Roz heard policemen out looking for her, imagined crazy bright blue flashing lights. She thought she heard a search party, combing the hill for her, the way they'd searched the mountain for Nate. She thought about him on the mountain, counting on people he didn't even know to come and save his life. Roz wasn't like Nate—she didn't want people to find her. She didn't believe other people came and saved you.

She clicked on the flashlight for the fiftieth time, and it cast big scary shadows against the sides of the tent. Would she ever fall asleep, and when she did, would she have a bad dream? She wondered if there was anyplace in Montclair where a person could go to fish.

She crawled to the flap of the tent, unzipped it, and looked out. There was nothing, and no one. She looked up, the way she had so many times in Jefferson, checking for the northern lights, but the Montclair sky was nothing like what she used to see in the North Country. There seemed no possibilities at all in what Roz saw when she looked up—a close, small, murky slab between her and whatever was beyond it. She crawled back inside her sleeping bag and huddled into herself and cupped her hands together and breathed on them.

She woke, in filtered tent light, in the same position, as if she had prayed the whole night through.

Eight

She knew, right away, where she was. She lay cuddled inside her bag, blinking, and listening to sounds that in the littlest bit of daylight were easy for Roz to recognize: birds, a few cars on the road. The voice she heard inside her head was just her own, telling her that she had lived through the night. She pulled herself out of the sleeping bag and onto her knees. As usual, the possibility of prayer tugged at her. She waited a few seconds to hear if God would speak this time, tell her what he had told Ellie, the very thing that led her away from the tent. It wasn't too late for God to tell her something, so she could know, but the only sounds were birds, and the traffic, picking up a bit.

She shoved wisps of hair away from her face and under the hood of her sweatshirt. Then she grabbed the nylon bag and started stuffing in her sleeping bag, punching the whole puffy mass of material down inside the little pouch. She could stuff forever—it seemed anything would compact and disappear when she pushed down on it and then pulled the drawstring tight.

The morning smelled early to her when she stepped outside the tent—too early for finding Nate at school. Why did so much of everything have to be waiting? She thought of the people at the bus station, watching their TV sets while they waited. She saw them just as she had left them, the same people in the same position, missing bus after bus, never getting where they needed to go. She peed, and got herself going.

The first person she met on the street—a sleepy-looking man walking two springer spaniels—told her that the high school was about a mile down the road that they were standing on. She found it hard to believe: that without a single turn or twist, she'd arrive at the place she'd been traveling to for so long. And when she did let herself believe it, the realization didn't flood her with relief. Closing in on what she was after pulled as well as pushed her. She thanked the man and started walking, but slowly.

Even holding herself back, Roz came to the high school quickly enough. She stood across the street and watched the entrance to the massive brick building, waiting, silent, like a dog. She watched intensely, undistracted, the way Joan watched a door that she had scratched on and wanted opened. For just a second, Roz let herself think about Joan, and then Mike. She wondered if he would make his run to Circle Donuts, like always.

Roz had never once considered tracking Nate down at his home. She didn't want to know that he had a life, on top of just being alive. What if his father came to the door? What if his mother did? All she wanted from Nate's life were the moments when he'd been lost, the ones that weren't in any picture Roz had ever seen. She wanted to look at Isaac's face when he realized that he was the sacrifice, to hear whatever words might have lured Ellie away from the tent. She just wanted the whole story.

The first groups of students began trickling in and entering the building. They looked not so much bigger as older to Roz, as if they ran the school instead of it running them, and she crossed the street and followed them inside. A sign on the door directed her: ALL VISITORS PLEASE REPORT TO THE OFFICE.

The women in the office were gathered at a copying machine in the corner of the room. One of them, with silver hair in neat waves, looked up as Roz walked in and said, "Yes?"

Roz's own voice surprised her. "I need to find Nate Thompson," she said, loud and perfectly clear.

The woman approached her, coffee mug in hand, steam rising up from it. "What grade is he?" she asked.

Roz hadn't figured on that question. She knew his age—sixteen—when he'd been lost on the mountain, and that was last year, but what grade did that make him? The woman with the mug was studying her.

"Nate's a senior," one of the other women suddenly called out, while Roz stood still as stone, not having answered. She let out her breath.

The school secretary reached under the counter and pulled out a thick bound book of computer printout sheets. She flipped through it to the "T's" and then licked her index finger and turned several pages one by one until she came to Nate's schedule. "Locker 1207, homeroom 402," she told Roz. She'd put the book under the desk and returned to her friends before Roz even had the chance to say thank you.

Roz went out into the hallway, spun around by how

easily she had been told what she needed to know. No questions, no nothing, as if she were suddenly, after all her waiting and anticipation, being propelled toward him.

Roz set off down the hallway, following the locker numbers toward 1207. They led her, in ascending order, right where she needed to go—as simple as following a recipe, ingredient after ingredient, until the steaming baked loaf was ready to come out of the oven. Roz felt inside her that nothing could go wrong and everything would happen, now.

She slowed down as she approached Nate's locker. The hallway was still almost empty, with just a few students congregated toward the far end. Roz studied locker 1207, the little silver plate on the olive green door, as if it might have something of Nate to reveal to her. And then she backed off from it, and plunked down against the opposite wall to wait. It might have looked extraordinarily confident—setting herself down in the hallway—but she had to do it: her legs were shaking, her whole body felt as if it might zing out of control, and sitting seemed the safest way to contain herself. Roz looked down so that she wouldn't have to see anyone looking at her, but she watched the patch of hallway right by locker 1207.

She waited in some sort of bubble, where she did not think, or even imagine. She registered the noises around her: the slamming locker doors, the laughing and talking—one girl called out, real loud, "Hey, Ficket, meetcha at three," and Roz could hear all that—but the silence she was sitting inside felt bigger.

She watched a big long pair of black sneakers approach the space in front of 1207 and stop. She willed them to keep going, to move on to the higher numbers where Nate Thompson's locker wasn't, but they stopped all the same. Roz could not budge them. Finally she lifted her eyes and slowly took in the whole boy: his tall, skinny body, the rose-colored T-shirt, the back of his head, bent down as he spun the combination to his locker. He looked strong enough to Roz, strong enough to have climbed a mountain and climbed back down on his own. She held her breath while she looked at the back of the boy her mother died for.

She could not move, but when he yanked a book off his locker shelf, gave the door a slam, and took off down the hallway, she was up on her feet and behind him in a second. She didn't have to will herself to rise and follow him. The plan she was part of did it for her: lifted her up and made her speak. "Nate?" Roz said. "Nate?" a little louder.

He stopped and turned around, looked at her. He was stringy tall; his blond hair was long in front and fell across one eye. "What?" he said.

"Are you Nate Thompson?" Roz said. Nate Thompson from Montclair, New Jersey.

"Yeah?" Nate answered, wary. When Roz did not immediately speak again, he said, "So?"

"I'm Roz. I'm Roz Jacoby," she finished. She looked down, at Nate's feet again—not intentionally, but as if she had the right somehow, having revealed who she was. He was the boy who lost three toes to frostbite. She looked back up at him and he was staring at her, figuring something, but not quite there.

"My mother," she started, and then stopped, because he got it. She could see that he got it, by the way his face fell—the way accumulated snow slid off their steep-pitched roof up in Jefferson: suddenly, entirely, baring everything. He went white.

"My mother," she started again, just to fill the silence, "was on the mountain—"

"She fell," he said. "The rescue, I know," he said. He shifted the book he was holding from one hand to the other. A bell fired a blast inside the building. Roz jumped as if it had jolted straight through her. Many more kids had flooded into the hall, but Roz hadn't noticed. "Lookit," he said, talking past Roz, "I have class." She knew he was ready to bolt.

Roz stood still and did not answer him. She could feel how much he wanted her to disappear. It was a force, almost, that she braced herself against, so that no matter what, no matter how much he wanted her to be gone, she would not become invisible.

"Listen," he finally said, "whatayawant?" He sounded annoyed, even as he tried to stay cool. But he wasn't— he was hot, his face a deep red now, almost pulsing. The difference between how he looked and how he sounded threw Roz; she wasn't sure which to believe. So she said what she knew about herself: "I have some questions."

"Aw, man," he said, dropping his head to the left as if some weight had suddenly come down on it. He pushed his hair up off his forehead. "Now?"

For just a second it bubbled up in her that it didn't have to be now, that she could wait—until his class was over, or school was through. But she *couldn't* wait anymore; she was through with that part of things. "Yeah," she answered him, "now. But not here." It was as much as she knew just then, that she was in the wrong place.

"Well, where?" Nate said, a little louder, a little more sure of himself. "I don't have all day."

He should never have said what he did, about not having all day. It clicked something on in Roz. It made her mad, and being mad was bigger than being nervous, or being unsure of what she had to say. She pulled up to her tallest self. "Outside," she said, and she led him down the hallway—against the tide of kids flowing into the building—down the steps, and across the street.

Roz made sure to walk fast, and stay a little ahead. All she was doing was getting them to a place that felt more on her side of things. She must have been walking very fast, because she heard Nate call out to her, "Listen, where're we going?" and she could hear that he was a little winded. She didn't answer, just kept walking, absolutely sure that he would follow.

When she reached the entrance to the park where she had spent the night, she stopped abruptly. Nate came up behind her and she wheeled around. They stood, breathing hard, face-to-face. She would take him back to the tent, she finally knew. "Up here," she said. He once again followed her as she led him to the stand of rhododendron bushes, and, through them, to the place where she had pitched the tent.

When she turned to face him, she could see that even though he had followed her, he was scared.

"What?" he said, before his breathing was back to normal. He said it the way he might have said, "I didn't do anything."

Without the motion of her walking, in the quiet of the park, Nate's question registered. "What?" What did she have to say? Nothing, no sound answered her. Roz knew she held the moment in her hand, that she could take all the time she needed, but nothing came to her. Nate shifted from foot to foot. As he moved, she grew more still, and even, it seemed, older and taller. She became perfectly quiet inside, listened to his breathing, the way she had listened when she telephoned him from the pay phone on High Street.

"I'm the one who calls," she finally said. "On the phone."

Nate did not look her in the eye, but scrunched up his face when she said that, as if he might not even know what she was talking about. "Yeah?" he said. "How come?"

She told him the truth. "I don't know." It was almost as if they were having a conversation. "I just had to, sometimes." She remembered the urges and how they would come over her, but it was like remembering a past life, or someone else's. She wouldn't need to do it anymore, she could already tell. It wouldn't even work, now that he was flesh and blood to her, a regular boy she'd laid eyes on. "I won't call again," she told him.

Nate shrugged, drew in the side of his left cheek, and started to work at it.

"Didn't you ever want to call me?" Roz asked him, next. She had never asked herself that question before, but it came to her now, all of a sudden. "Didn't you wonder about me?"

He pushed the hair away from his face. "Yeah," he said. "Sure. But I couldn't. They told me not to, they said it would be better . . ." He trailed off.

"Who?" Roz wanted to know.

"The lawyers, my parents' lawyers. They said we couldn't be in touch with your family in case of lawsuits or something."

Roz could not understand what she was hearing. Why was he talking about lawyers and lawsuits? What did law have to do with it? What laws were there about losing her mother, about being sorry? His words hit her like a little avalanche of mountain rocks.

And then she heard Nate say, "About what happened . . ." and those words brought her back to what she needed more than anything. She echoed him. "What happened? Tell me what happened."

"Like what?" he said. He finally looked directly at Roz. "You mean when I was lost?"

"When she found you," Roz said. "How she found you, and then when she fell."

He took a deep breath in and then pushed it out. His T-shirt stretched out and relaxed with his breath. "I was really out of it by then," he said. "I was freezing. I kept hearing people calling my name, but it was always just the wind. By morning, I didn't know if I was dead or what. I didn't know what was happening." He looked at Roz to see if he was sounding crazy. "Weird, huh?" Color had flooded his cheeks again, a deep pink.

Roz nodded fast, that she got it, and for him to go on.

"Then your mother came," he said. "Outa nowhere. All of a sudden she was just standing there, on the ridge above the ledge I'd fallen onto."

Roz drew in her breath. She was there with him, and she could see her mother. "Tell me everything," she said, begging.

"I thought she was an angel." He said it inside a laugh, as if it were stupid to say so.

But Roz answered, "Oh, yes," so quickly, and with such heart, that he said it again, dead serious: "I swear to God, I thought she was an angel."

"What did she say?" Roz asked. "Exactly."

"She said," and he began slowly, as if he were dragging

the memory up from a basement with steep stairs, but then he stopped. "She didn't say anything. I just saw her, and she saw me, and then she disappeared."

"Disappeared?" Roz said, ambushed. What kind of ending was that? The story could not possibly be over yet. She did not know enough. It was not what she had come for.

"Yeah," Nate told her. "She stepped back off the ridge. To make her way down to the ledge from the other side, I thought." He laughed when he said, "I was bawling," the way he had when he'd first called Ellie an angel. "I was so glad I wasn't gonna die. When she didn't show up again, I thought I'd dreamed her. I thought I was hallucinating."

"You didn't see her fall?" Roz said, trying to quell the panic that was rising up in her. She had crossed her arms across her chest and was digging her fingers into her arms.

"What?" he said. "No. She just stepped back, out of sight, and then I didn't see her anymore. I thought I dreamed her," he said again.

"Oh, God," Roz said, pulling her arms in even tighter against her and rocking back and forth on the balls of her feet. "Oh, God, oh, God." She could have been praying.

Nate pushed his hands into his jeans pockets and waited. He'd come off the ledge where he'd been lost, but Roz hadn't.

"You didn't hear a thing?" she said, begging for even a sound.

He shook his head. "There was still wind," he said, "and she had gone around behind me."

What did Roz want? What was it that she had to have or she might die? A scream? A word out of her falling mother's mouth? A sign that her mother meant to save Nate and then come back home, to the kitchen, to where Roz was waiting? Anything except silence and disappearing, just slipping away, out of sight and hearing. Roz could feel her own ears growing, straining to hear what Nate must have missed—surely there had been something. She thought her eardrums would explode from listening so hard, as hard as she had ever listened for God.

And the harder she strained to hear, the more nothing came back at her, until, finally, it was like being punched in the face with not knowing, not finding out. And when it hit her, that punch, she finally, absolutely, once and for all got it: that she did not know and she wasn't going to know exactly why, or even how, her mother died. Being hit so hard knocked out her straining to hear, and she just stopped, still as stone, still hugging herself.

"I'm sorry," she heard Nate say, and she realized he had said it before, because she was hearing it again. "I'm real sorry." Roz looked down at him. He had dropped down to the grass, kneeling, resting on the backs of his heels. Once she listened, *sorry* was easy enough to let in—smooth, warm, fluid, like a drink her whole body had been wanting.

He looked up at her from his squatting position, and she dropped down to his height, to be with him. She knew he was going to cry and she wanted him not to. If he started, so would she.

His whole face was working against his crying, taut and pulling at itself. "I'm sorry about your mom," he said, his voice at some in-between register that Roz did not know about. He reached out and grabbed a handful of grass and pulled it up.

"Oh, me too," she said, leaning on the "too," falling on it really, with such relief to be saying it. Neither of them cried, but Roz's throat ached. They both studied the grass. Finally Roz let out a stuttery sigh and said, "How's your foot?"

Nate did not entirely register what Roz was asking him. When he did, he pulled his foot out from under him and planted it in front of them, as evidence, and they both considered his black sneaker. "It's okay," he said. "No big deal."

They looked at it some more. Then Roz said the bravest thing: "Can I see it?"

Nate looked from his foot to Roz, and didn't say a word.

"Will you show me?" she said, again.

Nate's face was afraid.

"Doubting Thomas," she said to him. "Do you know that story?"

Nate moved his head back and forth.

"Thomas was a follower of Jesus," she began. It was her mother's voice telling the story, the flow and rhythm of her words. Her mother had a beautiful voice. "And after Jesus died on the cross, he was buried and three days later he rose up again from the dead. But Thomas wouldn't believe he had risen. He wanted to believe, he tried, but he couldn't bring himself to, not until he saw Jesus for himself, with his own eyes. Not until he touched the places where they had nailed Jesus to the cross, the wounds."

Nate was holding still, as if things could be dangerous.

"It's not crazy," she said. "Some people are like that."

"What," Nate finally said, "you mean like take off my shoe?"

"So I can see it," Roz said. She had a sense, inside her body, of how far she had come, and how long all this had taken. "So I can finally believe it happened."

Nate didn't look convinced, but he must have understood, at least a little, because he told Roz, "I still dream about it sometimes." He was confessing to her. "And I'm always real glad when I wake up and find out it was only a dream. But then I have to remember that it really did happen—even though I dreamed it, so it's weird, you know?"

Roz nodded, and waited.

Nate's face was pulsing red again, but he reached over his foot and tugged the laces apart. He yanked the sneaker off by its heel and it fell, heavy and awkward, between them. Then he peeled off his sock, and stretched back as he extended his foot toward Roz.

It was just a foot, of course—a long, white foot, with small marks across the top from the sock or maybe the laces, and with three toes neatly missing, three little stubs where three toes would have been. Nothing about it looked wounded. The foot looked as if it had been born that way, just another kind of foot.

It was very still around them.

"You can touch it if you want," Nate said. "Like that Thomas guy."

Roz looked at Nate and then reached her hand out and lightly placed her fingers across the top of his foot, over the stubs. It felt clammy against her cool and dry fingers, made her aware that her hand was lovely. She drew it back. "Thank you," she said.

He dressed in silence. There was a quiet between the two of them, because they had been intimate, and didn't know how to come back from it. When Nate had his sock and shoe back on, all Roz could think to say was "You better go," and, after a pause, "You don't have all day." They both laughed.

Nate didn't make any motion to move.

"I won't call you anymore," Roz said. Had she told him that before? She all of a sudden felt so tired, so utterly spent. She thought there was probably more she was supposed to do, more she was supposed to find out, but she couldn't make herself care. All she wanted was to stretch out on the grass and sleep.

Nate stood up and she made herself stand, too. Before Nate loped off, he said, "Yeah, well, see ya." Then he told her, "Thanks," and Roz said, "You're welcome." They sounded so polite, Roz thought, as if they were having a grownup conversation. But what other words were there, big enough for what they were talking about?

"Will you get in trouble?" she said to him, right before he cut out through the bushes.

"Trouble?" he said.

"You know, for being late. In-house suspension?" she said.

He smiled and shrugged, and it struck Roz for the first and only time that she liked the way Nate looked. "Nah," he told her. "They'll never even catch me," and he was gone.

Roz went immediately to the tent—warm and close from the morning heat trapped inside it. She knelt back against her heels and closed her eyes, and remembered how her hand had felt on his foot, how gently she had rested her fingers across the top of it. She was waiting for what had happened to hit—food to take away her hunger. She was waiting for forgiveness to flood her and set her free. Roz started to hum, all is forgiven, while she waited for the feeling to register inside.

It wasn't coming, though—the feeling. She wasn't getting quiet inside, or full. She felt an explosion coming. *Challenger* was taking off all over again, there were faces looking at her, asking her what happened. She spoke out loud right before she would have screamed.

Mom?

Now what, Mom? *Tell me.*

I listen but no one ever tells me anything. How am I supposed to get the story? You're the only one who knows for sure, but you're gone. You're not even here. I listen for God—I do, Mom—but it's always quiet. You said, it makes you crazy, not being listened to. Well, who's listening to me?

And I don't want to be crazy. We're not the same. I don't want to go off and leave people waiting, in the tent, on some ledge. It scares them, Mom, it really scares them. I was so scared, waiting for you. I pulled out my eyelashes.

And how was I supposed to tell you, what difference would it make? God called you. You said you were answerable only to God. I'm not God, Mom, I'm just Roz, I'm just this kid. You always told me Abraham's story, what God and Abraham did—what did it ever matter, what Isaac thought?

Nothing I thought counted. It was just your voice, and listening for God, but I never heard anything, and I'm sick of listening, my ears hurt. Use my heart if you want to talk to me, I can't listen anymore.

I want a regular life. I just want my paper route and Mike and Joan. And someone who could deliver for me a few days if I needed her to. I'm different from you, Mom; we're not the same.

I'm not scared of snakes. And they're not all around the riverbank like you said. I only ever saw one, and it didn't scare me. Snakes scare you, Mom, not me. We're not the same.

I didn't go up on the mountain. I never followed you. Maybe you fell. Maybe God startled you when he spoke and you lost your balance, you could have lost your balance. I can't be sure. You're the one who's sure.

All I know is what I did. I stayed in the kitchen and I waited. I couldn't move. I didn't follow you up the mountain, Mom. I didn't push you. I didn't push you, and I couldn't catch you. It was you on the mountain, not me.

Nine

Roz cried hard before she fell asleep.

When she woke up, a big man was leaning his body into the tent, his hand on her calf, shaking her. She jerked awake, drenched in midday heat. Even as she heaved herself away from him, moving crablike toward the back of the tent, she could feel how soaked she was, and her insides were rattling. She did not even know who she was.

Her terror seemed to scare him. "It's okay, it's okay," he said. "Take it easy." The words might have been Mike's, helping her back from a nightmare. Maybe she was having a nightmare. The man had a gun. "It's all right," he told her.

Roz drew up her knees and held them against her chest, her hands pulling them in tight, away from the man, but there was nowhere to go. She wanted to see everything for what it was, but, waking up so fast, she felt she had left part of her self behind, deep underwater, and that part couldn't rise up fast enough, not against so much pressure.

The man pulled back from her, as well, so that just his head and shoulders remained inside the tent. His gun disappeared. "Are you all right?" he said.

Roz nodded, her eyes big.

"Can you step outside?" he said, but not really a question. He pulled all the way out of the tent as Roz came forward, crawling out into the hot, bright midday sun. It was hotter than it had been all year, hotter than it had a right to be in mid-May. The light hurt her eyes.

Outside the tent, the policeman wasn't nearly as big as he had seemed inside. He had his hands on his hips and he squeaked when he moved—the leather of his belt, and the holster.

Roz had never been close enough to a policeman to hear him squeak, or see how heavy and black his boots were. They were all she saw and heard, now.

"Didn't mean to scare you," he said to her.

Roz did not answer.

"What's your name?"

"Roz," she said.

"Roz what?"

"Roz Jacoby."

"And what are you doing here?"

What was she doing? She was standing there, looking at him. She was shaking inside. She was doing nothing.

The policeman looked over at the tent and then back at her. "Where do you live?"

"Newburyport," she told him. It was the first time she'd ever said that was where she lived.

"Newburyport?"

"Massachusetts."

He nodded. "You alone?"

Roz nodded: of course she was.

"And why are you here? There's no camping allowed in this park, you know."

Roz was awake now. She was awake and being questioned by a policeman with a gun belted around his middle, being told she had broken rules she did not even know about. "I'm sorry," she said.

"Your parents know where you are?" he asked.

Parents. Mike. Mike did not know. She'd left him waiting. "How could they?" she said.

"Why don't you come on with me, then?" the policeman said. "Let's get your stuff." He motioned to the tent.

Roz pulled out her backpack and handed it to him, and then they walked through the bushes and down the hill, to the squad car parked against the curb. She climbed inside it, a criminal.

The moment was so awful to Roz that it made everything that had come before seem suddenly perfect in her memory: the bus rides, the information window, racing down the emerald hill, the high school on the very road, not even a turn, Nate's foot beneath her hand. Now the policeman was taking her wherever he wanted, and everything that had been fine, that had been so perfect, was ruined. Was she being arrested? Would she go to jail? Was that what her mother had risked for her? Her mother, to whom she had spoken in anger?

She felt as if everything she had been able to do on her own was being pulled away from her, a spool unwinding. She wanted to fling open the squad car door and jump out, back to before she had been found, but she could see herself just hitting the pavement and rolling, against traffic.

"How long you been camping out there, Roz?"

He startled her, calling her by name as if they were friends. She looked at him and watched the way he drove, like he owned the road.

He said again, "How long have you been camped out, away from home?"

Answering him made her refigure the time she had been away. "Since yesterday," she finally said: an inconceivable answer. She had been away forever. Mike had been waiting in the kitchen forever.

"Had anything to eat?" he asked her.

Roz glanced down at the cardboard container on the seat next to him. Coffee cup, and chips.

"Help yourself," he told her, nodding his head toward the chips without taking his eyes off the road.

Roz reached into the plastic bag and put a few curled chips in her mouth. They were dry and salty and the noise of chewing them sounded deafening to her. She tried to dampen them first and crunch quietly, but it didn't work: the roaring inside her head was still there.

"We're going to the station," she heard him say. "We'll notify your family where you are." He looked over when he said, "They're probably worried."

Roz stopped mid-bite and nodded.

When they got to the station, Roz asked if she could use the bathroom and Officer Robert Hanks—that was what the letters on his silver pin spelled out—pointed her down the hall. Roz surprised herself in the mirror: her face, though tired and white, didn't have her story written all over it. Someone could look at her and not know a thing about her life and everything that had happened to her. She stared at herself, looking for more to show than did, but it was just eyes, her hair, long and on its way to dirty, and the straight line of her mouth. Everything she knew, and didn't know, was underneath. In the hallway, Roz leaned into the water fountain and let the frigid water spill around her lips and trickle down her chin, and wished she could drink forever.

Officer Hanks sat watching her from his desk, waiting to make the phone call. When she had finally drunk her fill, she walked back over to him, and reeled off the numbers, picturing Mike's face, and the heavy black phone in the hallway, by the front door.

"And who will we reach there?"

"Mike," she told him. Who else? As if Joan could pick up the phone, the heavy receiver in her mouth, a big black bone.

"And Mike is . . ."

"My uncle," she said. "My mother's brother."

"Okay," he told her, dialing.

"Can I talk to him?" she blurted out. She hadn't known she was going to.

He looked up at her, and then held the receiver out to her across the desk. "Be my guest."

Mike answered on the first ring. His voice was stretched. Roz saw a rubber band pulled so far that it made her eyes close, waiting for the snap. She could hardly stand to hear it.

"Mike," she said, "I'm here."

"Where are you, Roz? You okay? Oh, Christ."

His voice scared Roz. She concentrated on her feet, firmly planted on the linoleum floor. She leaned her hand on Officer Hanks's desk. "I'm okay, Mike, don't be scared."

"Where are you? What happened?"

She paused. "I'm okay," she said again. "I'm here."

"Where the hell is here?" he said, loud.

"Montclair," she shot back.

"Montclair?" he said, and then, "Oh, Christ, Roz." She could see him running his hand up from his forehead and over his scalp, pushing hair feathers out between his fingers. "How—" he started, and then, "Why the hell—"

Roz wasn't giving him enough fast enough. She could tell that. She said, "I have round-trip tickets."

"Oh, God, Roz," he said. "You're all alone"—as if that were the very worst thing that could happen; and Roz wanted to prove it wasn't true, and so she said, "No, I'm not, there's a policeman here, listen."

Officer Hanks took the receiver and right away began giving Mike information—places and times that Roz would never have thought to say first. He stopped talking for a few seconds, as if Mike had broken in midway to say something, and then Officer Hanks started giving directions to Montclair.

So: Mike was on his way. Roz could almost feel it, Mike coming to get her, could feel his truck barreling down the road, chewing up the miles between Newburyport and Montclair.

As screwed up as things were, as much as it wasn't the way she'd planned it, it felt like food and water and a shower that Mike was on his way. Roz pictured Joan in the truck, too, the hot wind so strong against her face it made her squint, even though Roz knew Mike wouldn't bring her, not all that distance. He'd just come on his own, as fast as he could. Once he'd told her that in Vietnam the only thing that ever mattered was getting to the guys who were wounded. She remembered that he said it didn't have to do with being brave. Roz assumed it had to do with love.

She thought about him not even stopping for coffee, just gas, passing right by all the fast-food places, just to get to her quick. At least she wasn't shot. When he got there, she wouldn't be dead, or even dying. He wouldn't have to look inside her chest and see her heart, exposed. Maybe that would count for something. Not that he had sounded mad—he'd sounded scared. Still, Roz knew when he got to her there'd have to be some sort of reckoning. He'd at least want to know what had happened.

But how much more did she know now than before she'd come to Montclair? It wasn't as if God had spoken to her. The most Roz had found out was that there were things she'd never know for sure. That didn't mean it was all horseshit, though. She saw herself walking the wobbly stone wall that divided one field from another in Jefferson, and Mike was on one side, in the grass, and Ellie on the other, but Roz was above and between them, keeping her balance. Her arms raised up like wings to help her as she stepped from one stone to another along the top. She knew that even though the stones looked big and solid, when she put her weight on them they jiggled beneath her.

"How about a sub?" Another policeman was talking to her. "I'm taking orders," he told her. His silver pin said Vincent Pinnoli.

No one had ever come right out and said so, and Roz had never asked, but after the phone call to Mike, she knew they weren't going to arrest her. They just had questions for her, and after a while, being in the police station with Officer Hanks and Officer Pinnoli didn't feel much different from being in school, or meeting with Frank Kerchaw.

"Can I have tuna fish?" she asked. Mike would've gone for the meats, she knew—pastrami, corned beef, turkey.

"You got it," he said.

All she really had to offer Mike, that she hadn't had before, was what her hand remembered—Nate's foot. That was real, those three missing toes. Mike, on his way, that was real, too. Joan. Her paper route. She started a list, something she could add on to. Tuna with the works.

Officer Hanks played checkers with her, and then cards. He taught her solitaire. She passed hours that way. Roz imagined that they had a kit of things—activities— that they kept there at the station, for cases like hers: waiting children. She liked Officer Hanks, and he acted as if he liked her, too. He told her about his own kids, Katie Marie and Noel, five and three.

Before Mike actually appeared in the doorway of the room where Roz was waiting, she heard a crack— the main door pushed open so hard that it hit against the wall of the building. And then, a few seconds later, Mike reached the threshold, though Roz did not instantly recognize him. She had never seen so much of him, somehow—as if all the energy and urgency spiraling out of him, almost carrying him, had made him bigger. He got to her before she had even taken a step, and yanked her to him, inside a hug.

Roz could feel Mike's whole, big body vibrating, letting itself go and holding back in equal measure, battling itself, almost. She did not know what was happening.

Mike, crying? Why was he? Was it like that in Vietnam, when he got to the guys who were wounded? Why would he cry, when she was the one who had done everything, who had made the mess? But then she knew. She saw him, in the kitchen, waiting a long time, willing to give anything if only Roz was okay and on her way home. Her heart hurt so much for him that she cried, too. They just held on to each other, and after a few minutes Mike pulled back a little and said, "How ya doin'?"

"Okay," she told him, and it didn't feel like a lie.

They both laughed, embarrassed at themselves.

"I'm sorry," Roz said next.

He didn't seem to care about that. He only wanted to get her and get her home. She waited back on the same chair while he talked to Officer Hanks, while he signed papers. He got a copy of one of the forms, as if he were getting a receipt for Roz, and he stuffed it in his pocket and turned to her and said, "Let's go."

She hoisted her backpack and followed him. Though Roz still had the feeling that things had unraveled—the trip, her life—she felt good climbing into the cab of Mike's truck, just the smell, the feel of it. There was a full pack of unopened Life Savers on the dash and Mike handed her the roll before they were even out of the parking lot.

First they followed Officer Hanks's directions back to the park, to get Roz's tent. It was dinnertime, and the light was the same as the night before, when Roz had set up camp on her own, and stood at the top of the hill and missed Mike, and wanted things to be over. Now the hill loomed before them, not quite as emerald as it had seemed the day before. She led Mike to the stand of rhododendron bushes, as she had led Nate there that morning, and back to the pitched tent. They each dropped to their knees to pull up the stakes, back and front. Mike had big hands, long and tapered, like the rhododendron leaves. She watched Mike pull up the stakes, easy as pie, like they were toothpicks. They'd have the tent down in no time, faster than she ever broke camp with her mother. Mike was totally concentrated on getting the tent down, the way, when he was fixing something, Roz felt like he just went inside his hands, he became the work he was doing. It was the way her mother had been with bread. They were related, after all.

Mike stuffed the tent and dropped the stakes into the pouch. "All set?" he said. It was the first thing he'd said since they had arrived at the park.

"Yep."

They walked together, down the path, and out to Mike's truck. He tossed the tent into the back, and climbed in the driver's side. He got behind the wheel and became part of it, joined at the hands, leaning forward slightly, as if that extra inch might gain him something, get them home that much faster. He switched on the radio, but kept it low, and didn't jab at the buttons the way he normally did. Roz could tell that the trip—everything—had taken it right out of him.

Nothing like anger filled up the cab. There were just the low-volume commercials and music from the radio, and quiet between them. Actually, it felt more like shyness—not knowing how to get around that something big had happened. Roz thought she should explain, but Mike wasn't asking anything. She kept working on the Life Savers.

Roz popped the last orange one and promised herself that after she had sucked it down to the most fragile, thinnest O, and when it finally broke in her mouth, she would say something. "I was on my way home when the policeman found me," she finally started. She remembered how big, not even human, the hulking figure had appeared to her, in the tent.

Mike stirred in his seat. Roz could feel how uncomfortable he was, pained even—the way he'd been when they had first walked into Frank Kerchaw's office—and he didn't say anything, but Roz kept going. It was her story, after all.

"I had to find Nate Thompson, the boy on the mountain."

"Why's that?" Mike said, as if they were talking about something that didn't have anything to do with them, as if it were just local news.

Roz sighed. "You know doubting Thomas?" She got a sinking-down feeling as she said it, because it never carried weight with other people the way it did with her. How else was there to explain, though?

"Yeah," Mike said, "I know doubting Thomas."

"Well, I needed to see for myself. Plus I got all these signs to go do it."

"Signs?" Mike was staring ahead, at the road, and his voice was flat.

"Well, you know, I got my period"—she gave him a quick look, and then kept talking, fast—"and Nate's phone got disconnected, and all the dreams."

"What dreams?"

"The bad dreams."

"What about the dreams?"

"Dreams are a sign, Mike. I know you don't believe that, but I do. They were the first sign that I needed to go."

"Oh, Jesus, Roz," Mike said, and his wrists let go and his fingers held down heavy on the steering wheel.

"I know it's horseshit to you," Roz said, quickly enough so that he wouldn't say it first. She didn't want to hear Mike say that something was horseshit, didn't want to clench inside with his definite "sh" and "t," how sharp they sounded. So she was surprised, when she said it, how easily the word spilled out of her mouth, even how good it sounded to her.

He was still slumped down. "They're *my* dreams," he said.

Roz looked at him.

"They're my damn dreams," he said, again. "The nightmares, they're mine."

"No," Roz said, confused that he wasn't following her. "I mean *my* bad dreams, when you have to wake me up."

"That's what I'm telling you," he said, close to mad. "They're mine. I'm the one who has them. I wake you up when I have them."

Roz's mouth started to work, but nothing came out. She just looked at him, and he looked so miserable, his mouth twisting out at the edges, his hands holding the steering wheel so hard.

"I have 'em, you know. And they creep me out, so one time I just woke you up, for company, and I thought I'd just do it that one time, that's what I always think, that I'll do it this one time, and then I was doing it every time."

Roz still could not think of anything to say.

"What can I say?" he finally said, shrugging. "You're good company."

Roz couldn't have said how she felt about what she was taking in; she was still caught by the news that the dreams weren't hers. "They're your dreams," she repeated.

"Yeah," he said.

"What are they?" she said. Did Mike remember? She could never remember—but they hadn't been hers to remember.

"Just bad dreams," he told her. "Your basic sick shit. Scary. They wake me up and I gotta get outa bed, you know?"

"So I don't have any?" Roz could tell her questions were weights on Mike, and she didn't want them to be, but she had to understand perfectly.

"No," he answered her.

"And that's why I never remember them?"

"I would imagine so," he said, with a little laugh.

So now she was following, and she had to continue. "Why did you say they were mine?" She wasn't mad, she just wanted to know. Mike was the best shot at straight answers she'd had in her whole life.

"It was a bad move," he started. "I don't know. I hate having them. I felt bad waking you up. You're a kid, for Christsake, Roz, you need your sleep. School and everything. I'm a grown man."

He said it as if it weren't true—that he wasn't a grown man at all. Roz felt afraid for the first time. What was he if he wasn't a grown man, and where did that leave her? All the same, she had to go on with her questions, exacting whole answers while she could get them: "So you have bad dreams and then you wake me up and that helps you, to go downstairs and maybe go fishing?"

He nodded as if the truth were something unbearably sad.

"But that's good, then," Roz said.

"What," he said, flat.

"That it helps you. I mean, it's good if you have someone there to help you when you get scared. What's bad about that?"

He didn't say anything.

"There's nothing bad about that," she said, absolutely sure.

Ten

After she got back, Roz spent a lot of time upstairs in her room, on her bed. She kept her door shut, and her room grew warm, especially in the late afternoon. Occasionally the breeze lifted her curtain out, away from the window, and blew across her. She lay on her bed and did nothing, the way she used to spend so much time in the graveyard, just watching the clouds sail by.

There'd never been a spring like it, people said—such a run of perfect days: sun, a cool breeze, not even many bugs. The extended period of beauty wasn't lost on Roz. It had started, really, with her trip to Montclair, and just never stopped. She felt somehow responsible for the weather, as if she had unleashed it, and it was hinged to her and what she did or didn't do. After a while, the beauty began to weigh on her, and she wished that it would break, move on to summer and humidity and even mosquitoes, just get off her back.

She slipped back to school with no explanations necessary, because Mike had covered for her. He told them she was sick, when they called. And he hadn't notified the police, either. "You wanna screw something up," he told her, "bring in the authorities." She'd picked up her paper route as if the two days she left it hadn't happened. So things seemed the same, but they weren't. Nothing was settled.

Up in her room, on her bed, she thought about what it must have been like for doubting Thomas, *after*—after he'd put his hands in the wounds, when he knew, for sure, that Jesus had come back from the dead. How settling could that have been? It wasn't the end of anything, it was probably only the beginning.

But what did he *do*? She realized that it's not as if things stop once you get some answers. You think that what you want to know is all that matters, but what really counts is the asking, and, later, that you're willing to accept the answer you get, or even that you don't *get* an answer. And by the time you're there—willing—you're cracked open, you already believe, and there's really no going back, and no stopping. You find something out, and then you go *on*.

It came to Roz, one day, lying in her room, what was next. The understanding came whole and in an instant, as if some part of her had been working at the problem for a long time, growing an answer that, when it was ready, fell solid as an apple into her silent thoughts: it was time to bury her mother's ashes. There was nothing stopping her.

She brought it up to Mike a few nights later, after dinner, in the shop. She'd settled into the couch, Mike was working on a busted lamp. Practically everything on TV was reruns.

"I think it's time to bury Mom," she said.

Mike looked at her, then nodded slowly. "Okay," he said.

Roz wanted deciding and saying yes to be enough, but Mike had questions. "So how do you want to do it?"

"Do it?"

"A lot of ways to bury people, Roz," he said. He stretched the cord from the lamp taut. "Some of them nicer than others."

She had nothing to compare it against. Mike did. Some part of her knew he was remembering Vietnam.

"You can make a big deal out of it. You can keep it small."

Roz said, "Oh, it would be just us"—everyone who loved her mother, she thought.

"And what'll we do with the ashes?" he said.

"Well, we'll bury them, what else?" She remembered, though, as she said it, that you could scatter them. There had been talk, after the accident, of scattering the ashes on the mountain. The thought horrified Roz, flinging her mother out like that, having her fall all over again. She wanted her planted, contained, she wanted to touch the dirt herself. "Just you and me, and we'll bury the ashes in the graveyard, and put up a tombstone that says something."

He nodded again, both his big hands on the workbench. "You know what you want it to say?" he asked her.

Roz remembered the inscriptions she liked best at Oak Hill: LEFTIE. BORN TO DANCE. REVERENCED. A TRUE WOMAN. She liked the ones that let you know a specific person, someone who'd lived a real life, was there, underneath, and remembered.

Who could say if inscriptions told the truth, though? Maybe they told more about the people who chose them. Roz remembered the names people had called her mother. Crazy. Hero. Angel—words that the people who spoke them needed to believe. What they called Ellie changed even though Ellie stayed who she was. What if Roz changed, too, and understood more about her mother than she could know right now?

For an instant Roz imagined a blackboard, instead of a tombstone, over Ellie's grave. She could write in different words as she needed to, as they came to her. Every single rain would wash the slate clean. But no: then anyone could write on it, call her mother anything they wanted. Ellie's memory belonged in the hands of people who loved her—Roz's hands.

What were they, then, the right words? What *about* her mother? Roz thought of what she knew for sure: Ellie loved God. She answered God. She baked bread. Maybe she was an angel. Could you carve a *maybe* in stone?

"You know, it's not like you *have* to say anything," Mike told her when Roz didn't answer him.

Roz did, though. Roz did have to find words for her mother. Ellie deserved her story. "Is there such a word as 'pray-er'?" she asked.

"Yeah," Mike said. "Prayer."

"Not the thing you say, prayer. I mean the person—someone who prays, like Mom did."

He carefully threaded the electrical wire up through the body of the lamp, pinched it, and then looked at Roz. "No person, no prayer," he said. "Ellie *was* the prayer, her life."

What he said scared Roz. How could someone's life be the prayer? What—just the hours? fixing meals? sleeping? Where was God's voice in that? But Mike had said it as if it were the most obvious thing, as if he were telling her to plug in the toaster, or that dinner was ready. She wasn't scared because he had said it, she was scared because she had heard it. "I hate that stupid lamp," she said, out of nowhere, turning away from him and back to the TV.

"This?" Mike said, holding it out and looking at it as if for the first time. The base of it was white and sculpted to look like a gnarled tree, and a painted Chinese man sat beside its trunk. "Yeah," he said, "it's pretty ugly."

Wasn't it just like him to agree?

At the next commercial, Mike told Roz, "Look, whatever you want to do is fine by me. You let me know what you want and I'll take care of the arrangements. You call the shots. Okay?"

"All *right*," Roz said, crossing her arms, as if they had had a little fight, as if Mike were pushing her to do something she didn't want to, even though she'd been the one to bring it up. It was confusing. She was making her way in the dark, and part of her wanted to feel her way forward and part of her wanted to hold still, just lie across her bed and watch the breeze lift the curtain away from her window.

So she surprised herself—because it's hard to gauge how far you've gone in the dark, or even that you've moved at all—when she announced to Mike just a few days later that they might as well go ahead and look at some tombstones, and maybe order the flowers.

On Saturday, she and Mike drove to Miller's Memorials, out on Route 113, in between the Chinese restaurant and the auto repair shop. The selection of sample tombstones on the blacktopped driveway didn't do much for Roz. She walked into the damp coolness of the shop and asked the man who ran the place about angels.

"Angels?" he said. He was a fat man. "You get into freestanding angels," he told her, "and you're talking real money."

"How much?" Mike asked, from behind and above her.

"A grand, fifteen hundred easy."

Roz turned around and watched Mike's eyebrows shoot up, his hand slide over his scalp. Clearly too much.

"We could sandblast some wings, on the stone. Wings won't run you so much."

But Roz wanted the angel or nothing—her whole, full body, not just specks of dust blasted from the face of the stone.

Mike and Roz faced each other and whispered about the angel, as if they were in church, or telling a secret.

"You really think an angel's the way to go?" Mike asked, worried.

Why wouldn't he be? The cost was so high. Roz was amazed it was so high—she'd never even considered what the price might be. And how do you know what something is worth? It was only worth feeling good over, she decided, not bad. "No," Roz said.

"You sure?" Mike asked. She could tell he felt bad, knew he wanted to say, "No problem, get the biggest damn angel you want."

Whose idea was *angel*, anyway? It was Nate's word for Ellie, not Roz's, certainly not Ellie's. "I'm sure," she said.

"Okay, then," Mike said, "but you pick out anything you want for the flowers. I'm springing for everything."

"We just want a plain marker," Roz said to the man.

They chose the plainest stone he had, small and dark gray.

"And what about the inscription?" he asked them.

Roz was ready with her answer: Ellie's full name, Ellen Burns Jacoby.

"Dates?"

Roz didn't care about dates. They reminded her of history tests, seemed just a complicated way of figuring out how old someone was. "Do we have to?"

"However we do it is fine," Mike said, with such conviction that it was as if he were talking to someone else, about something else.

Roz felt almost embarrassed by how adamant he'd been. "Then just her name," she said, "her full name, and this." She pulled out the piece of paper on which she had written her final decision about the inscription. The man read it and then looked past Roz to Mike, for adult approval.

"Word for word," Mike said. As he wrote out a check for the deposit, he reminded Roz again that he was springing for everything.

At the florist, Roz stood next to the glass-doored refrigerator that held buckets of iris, birds-of-paradise, roses, freesia, and looked through a leather-bound book of arrangements she could special-order. She studied the pictures inside their plastic pages and tried to imagine each one perched on the mantel of their house in Jefferson, and her mother's face beside it. Roz was a little pulled by the cross made up of roses, thinking it had more to do with God, somehow—though she couldn't really think how, when it came right down to it. She hadn't grown up with crosses. Ellie never rested one on the mantel, alongside the things she found most beautiful. Roz remembered the treasures Ellie placed on the mantel: animal bones bleached white by the sun, a bit of honeycomb, stones, the season's first bouquet of wild-flowers.

"What about this?" Roz called out to Mike, holding up the book to see if the cross did anything for him, but, from over in the gardening section, he barely raised his head up from the spades and pitchforks. "It's your call," he told her. "Get the one you like."

She put the book down with a sigh. Mike was willing to take care of things, but not to act as if they mattered. Why did it have to be her decision when she could make the wrong one? She went through each of the pictures again, a little mad.

Finally she made her choice. "I'll take this one," she said, pointing to a large horseshoe filled with yellow mums resting on a stand that looked like an easel. A little glittery sign in curlicue script read *Good Luck*. "Without the sign, though," she said.

Roz liked that it was connected to an animal. And it was more of the country than anything else she saw.

Mike walked over to the desk, happy to pay for whatever she'd chosen. He glanced down to see what it was. "Good one," he told her. "Hey, why *not* get the sign. Everyone can use good luck."

But something about it struck Roz as disrespectful, and she said flatly, "No."

Mike pulled out his wallet from his back pocket and said, "You're the boss."

After they ordered the stone and the flowers, Mike bought a plot at Oak Hill and arranged for the caretaker to dig the grave, and they set a date and time. It felt to Roz as if all the things to do were dropping away one by one, and that soon there'd be nothing left. That week, she got her period for the fourth time, and she pictured her insides just letting go, emptying herself out. It wasn't bad, though—being empty didn't scare her. The feeling had more to do with starting from scratch, down to the bone so she could grow new skin. The emptiness let her know that she had room inside, for the first time ever. Room enough, maybe, to start a life. Sometimes it felt hungry, being that empty—not even having her own nightmares! But there was a certain lovely privacy to having so much room.

She lay on her bed for hours. The ideas—the pictures, really—for how she wanted the ceremony to be just appeared. More than listening, Roz was seeing things now. She could see that there would be kneeling. And walking, of course, since walking mattered so much to her mother. She and Mike would walk around the graveyard three times, in a loop, with Joan. She pictured them making their way along the path, and they were floating, almost, suspended. She saw them eating bread, too—she remembered from a place so deep it felt beyond memory: Ellie cutting off the end of the just-baked loaf, slathering it with butter, and holding it out for Roz to bite into.

Finally she wrote out a program for the ceremony. She had in mind the fliers they gave out at school band and chorus concerts, something to list the order of things. She took two pieces of paper and folded them in half. On the front of one she drew a bunch of flowers in a vase, and on the other she made several little drawings: a loaf of baked bread, with squiggly lines radiating out from it to show that it was hot and fresh out of the oven; a flower; a tent.

Inside both she wrote the order of the service as she saw it:

Walk (Going In)
Bury
Walk (3 Loops)
Eat Bread
Pray
Walk (Going Out)

She had planned on surprising Mike with them, but she liked them so much that she couldn't wait to show him.

"Eat bread?" he said, the first thing after he'd read it.

"Yeah," Roz answered, suddenly embarrassed. "You know." But how could he—know? He hadn't been there when Ellie made bread, cut off the end for Roz to eat. He didn't know how it felt, what it meant. And what words were there, really, to explain it?

He didn't need an answer, though. "Sounds great," he said, handing the order of service back to her, returning to the busted vacuum cleaner. Roz stood and looked at him. Anything she planned would sound great to Mike, she realized, as if there were no right or wrong way to do it, bury Ellie.

"I'll pick up some French bread at Shaws tomorrow," he told her.

"What?" she said, picturing the long skinny loaf, so unlike the fat, round, steaming bread her mother always offered her. "I was, um, thinking it should be baked."

"It will be," Mike said. "Just not by us." He looked at her. "Is that a problem?"

Was it? Roz didn't know. Maybe the home-baked bread

was just another angel, something to let go of. Baking it with Mike wouldn't be the same, anyway: Mike wasn't Ellie.

"No, that'd be good," she told him.

"I thought I'd make some deviled eggs, for after."

"Good," Roz said, and they stayed up late Tuesday night and deviled a dozen.

On Wednesday morning, after breakfast, Roz lifted the dress out of her closet that she'd counted all along on wearing. It was the only piece of Ellie's clothing that Roz had saved, her mother's favorite dress. Ellie had found it at a yard sale, hanging from the limb of a tree. "It's like a garden," she told Roz, clapping her hands together. It was: filled with blue and orange and rose-colored flowers. Roz had never seen her mother delight so much in something to wear. When she'd bought it—for two dollars, Roz remembered—it was as if she'd given them both a present.

Now Roz took it out and laid it across her bed: a flower bed, she thought. Then she stepped out of her shorts, and in one continuous movement pulled off her T-shirt and dove into the skirt of the dress, swimming into the bodice and sleeves. It didn't fit, though. It was too tight, as if it had shrunk, hanging in the darkness of her closet for the past year. She pushed her arms through anyway, and felt it stretch across her chest, pulling at the shoulders. She could barely breathe out. She stood inside the girdle of a dress and wanted to cry at what had happened.

Mike walked by Roz's door and looked in. "Hey," he said, laughing, "you look like a million bucks."

A laugh started up in Roz, but the impulse to cry was every bit as strong, and the two collided inside her.

"Looks comfortable as hell," he said.

Roz spun around and threw up her arms—maybe to tell him to stop, maybe because she just didn't know what else to do—and both shoulder seams gave at the back: a fast, tiny ripping sound that she felt all up and down her body. That did it, the slight ripping. "Shut *up*," she cried out, lifting her right leg and slamming it down onto the floor.

Her reaction stunned them both. Mike's eyes got big and rounder, his smile vanished—poof. At first he didn't say anything. Then, "I loved her, too," he told Roz evenly, and turned and went downstairs.

Roz pulled the dress off her, struggling out of it, yanking her arms back through the spindly sleeves, pulling so hard that she was panting by the time she got it off, hot and frantic. She dropped the dress in a heap on the floor and stood naked except for her underpants, looking down at it, the mess of colors and flowers and soft, old cloth. It was nothing, really—just a simple dress—but she had battled it as if her life depended on getting it on, first, and then off. Finally her breath became regular as she stood looking at it. She stooped down and plucked the dress off the floor and held it out in front of her. She examined the ripped seams in back. "It's just the seams," she could hear her mother say. "We can stitch those right up." Why hadn't Roz looked at it in the first place? It was obviously too small—she had grown way too much. She took it back to the closet and hung it up, where it had been before, and pulled down, instead, a cotton skirt and a rose-colored shirt. When she went down to the kitchen, whatever had happened between Mike and her had passed, and Roz knew the funeral service had begun.

At ten they stood in the front hall with the things they had gathered to take to the cemetery, their arms loaded as if they were going visiting and taking presents. Roz held the box of ashes she had lifted down from her closet shelf. Mike carried the bread, tucked under his arm, and the programs Roz had made. Mike had on his newest clean pair of jeans and a cotton shirt he must have bought for the occasion, Roz realized, with an alligator on it.

Roz whistled for Joan and the three of them stepped outside the front door into the sun. They began the short walk up to the cemetery, its arched stone entrance in sight from their doorstep. The maples on either side of the road made a lacy canopy over them.

Roz set the pace, slow and solemn, and even Joan didn't race on ahead. No one spoke. They could have been leading some strange procession, bearing gifts.

They walked beneath the archway and into the graveyard that Roz knew so well. They had the place to themselves, except for the birds. Mike had told her just where the plot was, and for the first time ever that Roz had walked there, she had a destination. She shifted her hands around the box of ashes and held it very carefully in front of her, giving it more support than it needed to be carried, as if it were terribly heavy.

They walked straight through the oldest part of the cemetery, past the little dip where Roz used to stretch out and watch the sky, and continued on toward the back of the grounds, where the newer tombstones stood, some of them not even filled: marked with names and birth dates only.

Roz grew sad as they left the moss-covered older plots, the ones that were so settled-seeming, as if the people there had grown used to being dead, belonged there somehow. The bushes and trees around them—azaleas, mock orange, roses—were full, and grown, in flower. Roz sank a little, approaching the sparser, more open area, closer to the road. She would so much rather have put her mother in the older section, where death seemed just a part of everything else around it, and beautiful really— not fresh and stripped and painful, the way it started to feel closer to the road. The sadness was flowing into her now, traveling through her bloodstream.

They came to the spot Mike had bought, the brilliant yellow mum horseshoe resting on its stand, the inscribed tombstone already set in place. All Roz saw was the hole—a small, neat rectangle had been dug out—with a mound of removed earth beside it. It stopped Roz cold, the actual hole. She stood and stared down into it and could not imagine what might happen next.

Mike set down the loaf of bread on the flower stand, and then opened and held out to Roz the order of service she had written. Roz drank down the words, thankful they were simple. So: they had walked (going in), and the next thing, the thing to do, it said, was bury.

Roz dropped to her knees—just a necessary act to bring her closer to the ground. Leaning down, she set the box of ashes on the bottom of the hole. She felt the coolness of the dirt, the solidness of it, as she let go of the box and it sat supported and still. Her hands, absolutely empty, remembered everything: the bread dough, Nate's foot, the beggar's hand, the whack of Scott's bone against her fist, the ache deep in itself. Her body remembered and knew what to do. She reached out and dragged down handfuls of dirt over the box. The earth felt wonderful to her hands, and she dropped mounds of it into the hole. It made a sound, of course: a dry, scraping sound as the earth landed and scattered across and around the box. She took comfort from the sound, the here and now of it, and the smell and feel of the dirt, and being on her knees. Pulling down the handfuls of dirt was as real as anything she'd ever done, at the exact moment that nothing at all felt real to her.

On his knees beside her, Mike was dropping mounds of dirt into the hole as well. When had he joined her? Neither of them made use of the stubby little shovel with the gold handle that had been placed beside the mound. They just used their hands, until the box was covered, out of sight.

Roz leaned back against her heels and straightened her back. All the sadness was inside her now and she surrendered to it, not giving up so much as just giving herself over to it—something that had been there all along, waiting to be let in. It washed through her in a wave that touched every part of her body, out to her fingers and toes, to the very top of her head, filling every inch, every breath of room she had inside her. Was that what she had made room for, all the sadness? She could feel her own heart breaking, the way the dress had ripped at the seams across her back. It was breathtaking, but when she finally exhaled—because she had been holding her breath—it was in an urge toward life, separate from her mother, and that was when the tears came, all in a rush, the breath and the tears, and the sadness pulsing all through her, at such loss. She felt close to drowning, in so huge a wave, but she was not drowning: she was crying, and breathing, in and out, in and out, solidly on her knees, not toppling over, grounded.

Moist earth clung to her fingers, and when her crying had subsided she looked down at the dirt all over her hands. There was no doubt she had done what had been next on the list: bury. She wiped her palms on the grass and rose up, as if some hook were pulling her up at the sternum and standing her straight, her knees locking back, her shoulders down. She had grown bigger, she could tell. As if her heart itself had grown, as if her whole body were her heart, beating, pulsing with sorrow. She was inches taller, and wider even, she'd made more room inside herself. She could never ever have worn her mother's dress. It would have exploded off her, flying apart at every seam, sleeves and skirt and bodice zinging out all over the cemetery, landing on the water tower, snagged by the tree branches. Thank God she hadn't tried to wear it, to fit inside against its will somehow, when it was much too small.

She stood and looked down at the grave, and then at what she had not seen when she first came in: the flower arrangement, big and yellow and surprising, and the small gray tombstone that marked the grave. She studied the letters, cut into the stone, of Ellie's full name. And below, in smaller letters, cut just as deep: ANSWERABLE ONLY TO GOD. She read the stone as if she hadn't chosen the words for it herself, and they interested her.

Mike, standing close by, brushed his hands against the sides of his jeans. Roz noticed for the first time that mosquitoes were out. She smacked one on her calf, and it spurted back her own blood onto her hand. "Gross," she said, extending her hand to show Mike. Then, without having to be reminded what to do next, they started walking.

Joan, who lay panting under a tree by the fence, sprang up and walked along with them, sniffing. Roz led. The same hook that had lifted her from her knees pulled her now, back to the path, and into the older section of the cemetery. It was a strong and faster walk, more their own than when they'd made their entry procession. Roz's body chose the route, which path they followed, close by the water tower, and then down by the place Roz used to watch the clouds sail by. It was hot: summer had busted through.

"Has it been three loops?" was the first thing Roz said. She didn't know, she hadn't been thinking, or paying attention, not in that way.

"Sure," Mike told her, and Roz knew, by the way he answered her, that he'd have said the same thing if they had walked around the graveyard three hundred times, or never taken a step.

"What next?"

Mike reached into his back pocket and pulled out the order of service, opened it, and read, "Eat bread."

They walked back to the gravesite. Roz stepped up to the wooden support for the horseshoe, where Mike had rested the long, narrow bag of bread. She hesitated, then took the loaf, reached inside the bag, and broke off a piece. It ripped away, soft and white beneath the crust. She looked at the chunk of bread and for a split second felt afraid—that what she was doing was stupid, that it didn't mean anything—but just as quickly, the feeling passed. She held out the bread to Mike and he took it in his big, wide hand. She pulled off another handful, dropped the loaf down in its bag, and set it back on the easel.

Then they just ate, stood there in the sun and crunched into the dry bread, unbuttered, and swallowed it down. Roz looked at Mike and loved what she saw: Mike, just standing there, chewing away, his mouth open a little, the same as at dinner. He smiled at her, shrugged his shoulders, took another bite.

When they were done, Roz dropped to her knees again, and Mike followed.

She closed her eyes, to have it dark. She didn't think about anything. No words, not one, came in or out. She could feel the bottom of her heart.

"Okay?" Mike said to her, when she opened her eyes.

"Okay," she said, and they stood up. Mike reached over and picked up the horseshoe and placed it on the grave, so that it framed the hole, and then they walked out to the blacktopped path and headed home.

They stepped into the dim front hallway and Roz felt her whole body give way to its coolness. She took three steps into the shop and plopped down on the couch. She felt as if she'd been riding some train forever, ever since her mother died, and as if the train had made one big loop, and finally dropped her back home, into the day, this particular, real day, a Wednesday.

Mike leaned against the doorframe. "Hungry?" he asked.

She remembered all the food in the fridge—all those deviled eggs. "Not very," she told him.

"Yeah," Mike said. "Me either." He didn't move from the doorway, and after a minute said, "How about some popcorn?" Popcorn was what they had when no one was hungry.

"Good." Roz couldn't follow him to the kitchen, though. She stayed on the couch and listened to him out there, dragging the heavy pan from the cupboard, grabbing the jar of kernels, pulling open the fridge to get the butter. Roz kept thinking, listening to every sound she knew so well, that she'd get up and join him while he made it. She could help, or she could lean against the sink and keep him company, but she didn't. She was still thinking about getting up when Mike walked into the room with a bowl overflowing popcorn cradled in the crook of his arm, holding two tall glasses of ice water, and the salt shaker.

She reached up for the bowl and set it on the couch between them.

"Wanna see what's on TV?" Mike said—almost shyly, as if maybe they shouldn't go back to their regular lives so soon. But it was all Roz wanted just then. She handed him the clicker and he turned on a wildlife show— birds—and just left it there, didn't even cruise the tube.

"Is there something we're *supposed* to do?" Roz asked.

"About what?" Mike filled his big hand with popcorn and then chewed right down to his palm.

"To end it, some way so you know it's over?"

He finished his mouthful. "This is it," he said. "Popcorn, and eventually bed." His voice was gravelly and certain. He'd said exactly what Roz wanted to hear.

"Good," she said, "then I'm gonna change." She wanted to be back in her regular clothes.

"Me too," Mike said, and they both went upstairs and changed into their shorts and T-shirts, and then came back down and ate all the popcorn. The birds were over and they switched to a Fred Astaire movie. Mike asked her if she wanted anything else, and she told him no.

Finally all she wanted to do was go upstairs and lie across her bed. "I'll be in my room," she told Mike, and he nodded at her. He'd made his way over to the workbench, was fiddling with a vacuum cleaner. "Thanks," she called to him, from the foot of the stairs.

"You too," he said back.

Her room was hot, but she didn't mind. She didn't mind anything. She fell across her bed and closed her eyes. Nothing was over, she knew. Everything mattered. She spread her arms wide across the sheets, and it felt like heaven, it felt like a million dollars.